The chilly grandeur of their tall Geo⋯⋯ ⋯⋯ ⋯⋯ the person Martina had become. Af⋯⋯ ⋯⋯ ⋯⋯ years of marriage, could she not behave more naturally? While her husband Robert preferred a cosy fire in the basement, Martina's decorous, mannered figure was acting out a dangerous fiction on the floors above.

She accepted that her daughter could not love her, but at least Louisa would grow up her own woman – not cowed, as Martina had been, by imperious in-laws. No one realized how deeply Robert's family had wounded her with their disregard – or what contempt now festered behind the careful façade of Martina's domestic virtues.

Ita Daly tells a transfixing story which explores the tenuous boundaries between passion and hostility, sanity and madness, that may be crossed without warning in the midst of family life.

Dangerous Fictions

ITA DALY

BLOOMSBURY

First published in Great Britain 1989

Copyright © 1989 by Ita Daly

This paperback edition published 1991

The moral right of the author has been asserted

Bloomsbury Publishing Ltd, 2 Soho Square, London W1V 5DE

A CIP catalogue record for this book
is available from the British Library

ISBN 0 7475 0715 5

10 9 8 7 6 5 4 3 2 1

Printed in England by Clays Ltd, St Ives plc.

To the memory of my mother,
Anna Daly

1

The necklace was a present from Robert, like so many of her possessions. It was a pretty thing, the flourish of the gold letters suggesting a Celtic influence, but she seldom wore it. It wasn't only that she didn't like the idea of walking about with her name depending from a chain around her neck; it was also the name itself.

Nobody was called Martina – nobody, that is, except for the occasional tinker's child or some Middle-European tennis player. It was the sort of name that warned the world that you were beyond the pale, over the top – a social absurdity. She should have had it changed years ago by deed poll. Before she had moved on. Before she had met Robert, who was never called Robbie or Bob or, most noisome of all, Roibeárd.

Martina sighed and dropped the necklace back into the bowl on the mantelpiece. The point was – and she must keep this in mind – the point was that there were several letters to be replied to, orders to be filled, lunch to be cooked, and all before twelve-thirty when Charlotte was arriving. If she didn't keep this in mind she would find the morning gone and her thoughts submerged, having strayed into those murky waters where they must never be allowed to wander.

It happened if she didn't keep a strict control on herself, especially on pale autumn mornings like this one with its attenuating echoes. She could find that several hours had passed as she sat becalmed, her mind locked in a no-man's-land somewhere between the past and the present. When she came out of this trance – for it was a kind of trance – she would feel both depressed and exhausted. She would look down at the hands in her lap and wonder whether she had the energy to raise one to smooth back her hair. It could be the best part of a week before she had recovered her spirits and was herself again: busy, purposeful.

Now she rose to look at herself, seeking reassurance. She was still beautiful – pale and misty like the October morning. There was nothing modern about her face; it was out of fashion with its high bare forehead, its lidded eyes. It was the sort of face that Piero della Francesca had liked to paint: inexpressive, slightly bovine because of its lack of animation. She looked better now than she had twenty years ago when she had had her hair cut across her forehead and worn her skirts halfway up her thighs. Now she didn't even show her calves and her hair was drawn back in a chignon worn low on the neck.

Thank goodness she didn't look like a Martina, anyway. She smiled at her reflection, then turned towards the window. Down below, Michaelmas daisies and bronzed chrysanthemums still bloomed, but the garden already had a cringing hang-dog air. She would have to begin an autumn tidy-up; tomorrow, perhaps, when Charlotte had come and gone.

'I should like to come to lunch next week.' As usual, Charlotte had invited herself. 'Wednesday suits me best and you can tell Lou that I've got something for her. She's such a mercenary little devil, that might persuade her to stay in and see her old grandma.'

Louisa had tossed her head. 'No chance – I'm having lunch in town. And really, she should realize that I'm past the age of bribing with lollipops.'

Martina had gazed admiringly at her daughter as she sat eating marmalade from a spoon. She was more like her grandmother than she knew, pleasing herself with smiling indifference, raising an impatient eyebrow at her mother's stricken face.

'I've no intention of putting myself out for her – you know she's a horror, Mother. I can't see the point in pretending that someone is pleasant just because they're ancient. When I'm her age, my grandchildren will want to come and visit me because I'm so sweet and charming, not because I'm offering them bribes. And . . .' She returned to the kitchen for her parting shot, 'She has begun to smell.'

Martina could deny none of this, though the smell was an intermittent one, coinciding, she believed, with Charlotte's drinking bouts. The whiskey, apparently, had a deleterious effect on her bladder and, when she came to visit them after a day on the bottle, Martina had noticed that the Givenchy did not quite hide the occasional whiff of stale urine. It was an old people's smell; you got it even in the poshest of geriatric homes and it seemed sourer, more penetrating, than the smell given off by wet nappies.

'Get her to change her knickers, why can't you,' was Louisa's final remark this morning. 'I mean, the way you go on about my friends and they only smell of sex, not piss.'

This was meant to shock and it did. It was the brutality of the language rather than the thoughts expressed. 'Knickers', 'sex', 'piss', were all words which made Martina flinch. She would find euphemisms for them even as she laughed shamefacedly at her own squeamishness. She found the expression 'making love' particularly silly, and yet she would use it as the only acceptable way of describing the act of copulation.

'Middle-class mealy-mouthedness,' her husband and daughter would shout derisively – and they would be right. She was stuck with it, though, just as she was stuck with this silly name of hers.

Martina, leaving the drawing-room, descended a flight of stairs to her bedroom. The house in which she lived was situated on the eastern side of one of Dublin's languishing Georgian squares. It was tall and narrow and pretty. The walls were painted green or grey and the polished wooden floors were spattered with rugs that surprised one with the brilliance of their colours when light from one of the long windows fell upon them. People described it as a restful house but remembered to wear an extra layer of wool when they visited. Those tall windows sucked heat from the rooms and corridors; the walls rose towards ceilings distant as Gothic spires.

Friends commented that Martina never seemed to feel the cold, and so seldom did she sit inertly that this was true. Robert, who hated the house, had inherited it from an uncle of his. Because Martina loved it, he had years ago resigned himself to living there, but insisted on his own rooms in the basement which, though darker than the rest of the house, was less chilly, and not merely because it was easier to heat.

The house was Martina's passion, the only one which she nowadays acknowledged to the world or to herself. She particularly loved it at moments such as this when it was hers and she could walk from basement to attic knowing that there was no one else there, that she was alone inside its sturdy, aged walls.

'I can't afford servants, you know,' Robert had said fourteen years before, when his uncle's will had been read. 'If you insist on living there, you'll have to keep it yourself. And don't expect me to spend money on painters, either – you'll just have to live with Uncle Bart's taste.'

This had been shortly after the scandal, when Robert's income had been halved and the sensible thing would have been to sell the house, even though the property market was depressed. Martina had pleaded. 'Let me keep the house, Robert – I'll do all the decorating and it won't cost you a penny, I promise.'

It took five years to finally eradicate Uncle Bart's taste. Five years of painting each room, of filling cracks in those impossibly high ceilings. She had sanded floors, stripped paint, replaced window sashes. She had removed stains from marble mantelpieces, she had rubbed and polished brass that had been tarnished for decades. She had made all the curtains and cushions and loose covers for the furniture, and when she was hanging the last pair of curtains she suddenly thought: I can make money from this.

The number of replies she got to the small ad placed in an evening newspaper surprised her. Nobody, it seemed, was capable of making their own curtains or willing to pay the exorbitant prices the shops were demanding for such a service. Within two months Martina was turning away twice as many clients as she was accepting and Charlotte was commending her practicality.

4

'It's the only way, Martina,' she had said, scrutinizing a hem. 'In today's world everyone must work – look at my girls. Although . . .' Her long face lost something of its severity. 'That is not really the same, I suppose. Artists *must* express themselves and those girls are truly artistic.' She patted Martina's shoulder. 'But you've a strong practical streak, my dear, and you can offer Robert just the sort of help he needs at this trying time. Keep it up.'

Charlotte was less pleased when Martina was taken over and became the junior partner in Co-ordinated Interiors. Freda Armstrong had come upon Martina and had instantly recognized two things about her: she was highly talented and badly in need of packaging.

She soon persuaded Martina that the killing was to be made at the upper end of the market and that she should be charging more, not less, than the fashionable department stores. The world, she assured her, was full of timid wealth which delighted to be bossed around as long as the payment was stiff enough. Thus was the ego protected and the truth confirmed that money hired and fired and was ultimately more important than either breeding or taste.

Freda was clever: she cherished Martina and saw to it that she was consulted and deferred to. Martina might be at home sewing but Freda made it quite clear that she did not consider her as any species of home-worker. So neither could Charlotte. Reluctantly, she had to admit to her daughter-in-law's enhanced status and now her insults became insults of commission.

From the first day that Robert had brought Martina home, a shy and pretty girl all smiles and ready agreement, it seemed as if Charlotte had difficulty in actually seeing her. Martina was certain that she had changed over the years, becoming less malleable as time went by, but Charlotte hadn't seemed to notice: her daughter-in-law remained invisible for most of the time, only popping into her line of vision in her role as wife and mother. Being forced to recognize Martina's success as a business woman made Charlotte cross, and she began to treat her with the sort of polite abuse that she reserved for her friends. This behaviour was not consistent, however, and gradually became more intermittent. Nowadays, most meetings with Martina had once again become occasions for Charlotte to talk about her son and granddaughter and about the Glory That Was Persse.

And would be soon again, now that Louisa was nearly grown up.

Though Martina had a business partner and a family, she had few friends, and those few viewed her with mixed feelings, considering her cold and bloodless. Robert admired his wife and was a little afraid of her. Louisa, who believed that her mother did not love her, had been trying for years to return the compliment and often went to sleep, her fist in her mouth, muttering, 'I hate her, I hate her. I always will hate her.'

Martina, seeing a daughter who grew tall and straight and self-centred, felt the terror round her heart loosen a little. Louisa would be all right.

Charlotte arrived now for lunch full of good humour. Robert had phoned her that morning from the gallery which she always took as a sign of his need to talk to her alone.

'I'm not surprised to find that Lou has gone into town – I didn't really expect her to stay in for me,' she said, waving away the sherry decanter and demanding Perrier. 'The young find the elderly boring – it is the way of the world. Besides, Lou can get away with such behaviour. She has the family charm.'

'She may be back soon, she just — '

'Nonsense – she's escaped. I'd have done the same at her age. I do the same today, for that matter. You won't find me at home when that awful woman downstairs invites herself up.'

Martina took this to be a reference to the rather timorous widow who had bought the ground floor of Charlotte's converted house.

'You look very well, Martina.' The tone was accusatory. 'I

suppose you and your friend have been rushing around, as usual, changing the colour of people's walls.'

'As a matter of fact — '

'It amazes me where they get the money, but, of course, I must remember we are the new poor. One forgets the extraordinary facility some people have for making money. Look at the success of your venture.'

Martina didn't bother to answer. She had discovered years ago that she couldn't compete with Charlotte in the subtle exchange of insults. When she had tried, she had sounded crude and bad mannered, unlike Charlotte who had perfected her technique.

'When I was a girl, people were content to live in the house they were born in and leave their walls alone. I'm sure it comes from America, all this desire for change. I don't understand it myself, but then, I don't understand Americans. With them even the old must be new. You must try to explain them to me, Martina – you are so clever about those things.'

With a smiling face, Martina offered her mother-in-law some more fish. Mentally, she checked – her neck, her shoulders, her jaw – all relaxed. Her heart-beat was regular, the blood was not pounding at her temples. She had grown her extra skin with great pain and persistence over the years but now it was complete. Don't feel, withdraw: if you don't feel anything, then you can claim not to have been insulted.

She also had the satisfaction of knowing that her calm indifference needled Charlotte.

'There is something innately vulgar in the desire for constantly changing the colour of one's drawing-room walls. It's a sort of – visual incontinence.'

Martina wondered how she had the nerve to use that word.

'And it's begun to affect people's conversation – have you noticed? When I'm asked out to dinner nowadays, more often than not I have to listen to someone telling me where I can get bargains in paintbrushes – it is unendurable. Mind you, I don't suppose you would know anything about that sort of thing, Martina. I'm sure your Americans don't have to worry about the price of paintbrushes.'

Since Martina had got the contract to supply the American Embassy with new curtains two years ago, it had become one of Charlotte's more persistent fictions that all of her daughter-in-law's social life was spent among Americans.

'Tell Robert to come and visit me – I haven't seen him for weeks. I could give him supper some night when you're busy. And give these to Lou. You can tell her I said that she doesn't deserve them.'

The necklace and matching ear-rings were of jet: pretty, probably valuable. Louisa, who never wore jewellery, would throw them in a box and forget about them. Her grandmother knew this and yet she gave her baubles, doling them out like the sweets that had caused so much trouble when Louisa was a child.

Martina, with her own filled and crooked teeth, had determined that her daughter's would be perfect. On this occasion, she had stood up to Charlotte. 'Please don't bring her sweets every time you visit, or at least don't give them to her. We only allow her to have them on one day each week. So if you wouldn't mind, Charlotte.'

The sweets had not been produced again and Martina thought she had won. Then, as she was putting her to bed one evening, Lou had asked, 'What's essentric?'

'A bit odd, unusual. Why?'

'It's what Grandma says that you are, not allowing her to give sweets to me, her darling only grandchild.'

'Do you mind?'

'No, because she gives them to me anyway, only secretly. Oh!' She covered the contentious teeth. 'I forgot I wasn't to tell you. It was to be our secret, Grandma's and mine.'

In those days, Martina used to go to Robert. He, busy and preoccupied, had patted her shoulder and said, 'Now, darling, you mustn't let Mother bully you. Louisa doesn't – she can stand up to her and she's only five.'

Yes, because Louisa was a miniature Persse and thus worthy of respect, more of an equal even at that tender age than the beautiful and alien creature who had lured into matrimony Charlotte's only son.

'You can't expect me to ring up Mother and remonstrate with her every time she does something outrageous – I'd have time for nothing else. I've told you, Martina – all you need to deal with Mother is a thick hide and a sense of humour. See if you can do something about developing those.'

Who was that girl who had run so beseechingly to hubby? Martina felt no affection for her nor regret at her demise. The woman she was today she was proud of: in control, invincible. Even lumbered with a name like Martina, she had come through; she had survived to endure luncheons with her mother-in-law and even to enjoy the food.

She began to load the dishwasher. When she had tidied up in here, she would spend an hour in the garden. There was sewing to be done but she must have a portion of pleasure. She would cut and clip and turn the earth. If enough leaves were down, she might make a bonfire. With no neighbours on this side of the square it did not seem anti-social, and, besides, she loved the smell of burning leaves. When she threw back her head and sniffed up the acrid scent, she experienced a sort of sensual transportation. It wasn't that she remembered in any intelligent or sequential fashion; it was more that for perhaps ten seconds she *was* fifteen once again. She was standing in a park in autumn smelling the burning leaves and for those ten seconds her body was shaken with the joy and excitement of possibility. The melancholy of the late afternoon park, the dreariness of the suburban road outside it, the lumpiness of her school uniform were as nought under the brightness of the knowledge that beyond lay the world waiting to be conquered.

She changed her shoes and let herself out by the back door. On either side of her tall houses rose. Inside, typewriters clicked and telex machines rattled inaudibly. Behind glass, secretaries and typists laughed. At desks, serious-faced men in dark business suits made wise and foolish decisions, making and breaking lives with equanimity.

In Martina's garden the soil was ancient and fertile. Plants, nourished by it, fought and flourished in the polluted air. A row of nerines was just coming into bloom. As the days shortened, they alone would splash their colour against the darkening shadows of winter. Within weeks, this garden would have changed completely, becoming bare, skeletal. All lushness and colour would disappear but it would still be beautiful in branch and stem. That was when Martina loved it most, when the air stung her cheeks and the closed office windows grew opaque with expelled breath. She responded to its austerity, to the weight of winter hanging over a city which seemed surely doomed. It justified her own excesses of temperament while acknowledging and reinforcing her ineradicable melancholy. She felt less depressed at such times than when the sun shone in a frivolous summer sky. She was a child of winter, of fires and toast and drawn curtains and lighted lamps. She sighed with pleasure now as she saw signs of its imminent arrival. She knelt and plucked at vegetation which came away in her hand, already rotten. Any day now . . .

2

Robert let himself in by the area door and passed down the corridor, flicking switches. Although it was sunny outside, no sun penetrated this basement, gloomy despite the bright yellow walls. To Robert it was preferable to what he thought of as the public part of the house, those large rooms upstairs, anachronistic and showy. How Martina could sit in that drawing-room beat him. And yet she did – staring down at the garden or reading a newspaper or drinking a cup of tea. When Robert went searching for her, he would find her there, marooned on the square of golden carpet, a waif astride a stiffly upholstered chair. At such moments he forgave her all the nonsense she went on with, her coldness, her bossiness. When he opened the door on her unguarded face, he saw the features relaxed in lines of melancholy, the eyes looking out blankly, sadly. At such moments he was overcome by pity and a sort of fear as he tried to reconcile this creature with the beautiful, coolly poised woman who faced the world.

He did not often allow himself to think of Martina; he hadn't the strength to look into that can of worms. There were certain truths about her, however, which he had to acknowledge, which were part of his vision of her. She was not a good mother, or at least not the right one for Lou. Robert loved his daughter but he knew that there was an emptiness at the centre of her life which he could not fill. He had watched her withdraw herself, close herself in like a hedgehog, so that, if one looked now, one would see only a brassy, careless teenager, one of today's youth, teetering on the edge of delinquency. But this was for outward show, Robert felt,

11

offered particularly to her mother. It was Louisa's way of dealing with her belief that her mother did not love her. Robert thought she was mistaken in this belief but he could no more convince her of this than he could persuade Martina how wrong she was in her approach to their only child.

Martina was acting a part – or was she? If she was, she had certainly perfected every nuance of her role. She never slipped up: she never slouched, never gobbled her food, never made an unconsidered remark or an unkind one; never raised her voice in anger, used a vulgar expression or gave voice to a vulgar thought. It was as if she was playing the part of some old-fashioned dramatist's conception of female perfection. Her manner and her manners were distinctly pre-war, reminding Robert more than anything else of archive film of those female announcers in the early days of BBC Television. And yet, could one keep up a role throughout the long years of marriage, throughout the yawns and excitements, the dull afternoons and shining mornings? Perhaps in the early days . . . If only he could remember more clearly.

He stooped to plug in a fan heater. They hadn't yet turned on the central heating, for Martina believed that the weather was still too fine. Throughout the house, however, Robert could feel an autumn chill.

He poured himself a whiskey and stretched his legs. He was glad to come home and find the house empty. The gallery had depressed him today, the puny talents that hung on the walls around him seeming to lock him inside a world of mediocrity. Most times he didn't even notice, but today the sun had been shining and, walking back through the lunchtime crowds, surrounded by chatter and easy laughter, he had been struck by the futility of his working life.

He would go back and spend the afternoon looking out the window or rearranging his pathetic little box of files. Rarely did a customer darken the door – the bright and fashionable young people who passed by outside would go elsewhere if they wanted to buy a picture. He had to laugh when he thought that some twenty years ago this street was being dubbed the new Left Bank. Other galleries had followed his and at one stage there had been five on this side of the canal. These had long since gone, of course, and been replaced by boutiques and swop shops; the pub on the corner still remained, but now at lunchtime it served chilled white wine, avocado salad and ripe Brie.

He objected to none of this – indeed, he often enjoyed lunch in that same pub. But today, in the autumn sunshine, he had wished suddenly that his life had not been such a flop.

So he was glad of this time on his own: he wanted a chance to gather himself together before Lou came bounding puppy-fashion on to his knee; time to make himself ready for the stilted ritual with Martina.

'How was your day, Robert?' A glacial kiss.

'Fine. And yours?'

'Not too bad. Would you like some tea?'

'The whiskey is fine.'

'Supper will be ready at seven.'

As if it were ever ready at any other time; as if they ever unfolded their napkins at any hour other than seven p.m. precisely.

Then frost would harden round the edges of the pine cupboards and poor Lou would bend her head miserably over her plate.

'She doesn't love me, Dad.' They had this conversation weekly. 'Being kissed by her is like being kissed by some sort of reptile. And has she ever slapped me or even given out to me properly? No. Because I'm not of enough interest to her for that.'

What did interest Martina? Robert believed the answer to that would, strangely, have to be sex. Her sexual appetite had always surprised him but, unlike other personality traits, it had always delighted him too; and it showed no signs of diminishing over the years. It was not that she was voracious; merely healthy and apparently uninhibited. They made love regularly, or, considering Martina's business-like approach, it might have been more accurate to say that they had sex. There were no kisses, few cuddles, no terms of endearment. There was much

13

enjoyment and consideration on both sides, and, on Martina's part, inventiveness. Afterwards, it was she who turned her back and fell fast asleep. Sometimes Robert wished for more tenderness, wished that Martina would lie in the crook of his arm and they could have those intimate, desultory chats that he seemed to remember from the early days of their marriage. Sometimes he wondered fleetingly if it would make any difference to Martina who it was she had lying beside her. For the most part, however, he was grateful to her for the pleasure she gave him, believing himself to be lucky in a wife who thus joyously reaffirmed her commitment to him and to their marriage. And this was what it was, this fleshly avowal. Wasn't it?

The sweetness of their sexual life was a consolation to Robert where so much else had let him down. Last week, he had come across a letter which he had written to Martina before their wedding. He had come upon it while searching through a cupboard for some old photos for Lou. He didn't know whether Martina had kept it or whether he had never sent it, but, as he read it, he felt himself blush.

He would always love her, he promised Martina. He would protect her and look after her. He would build them both a little nest, where they could retreat to, against the world.

He had torn it up quickly and stuffed the pieces in his pocket, fearful that Martina might come in and catch him red-handed. A nest – not even a peregrine falcon would choose to live in this house. And as for protection, how had he ever imagined that she needed it? Or had she, at one time?

Curiously, he could not remember. He had no difficulty recalling his school and college days, but his early life with Martina was a blank. He couldn't remember how she had looked or sounded, if they had done things together, gone places, talked to one another, something they certainly hadn't done latterly. It was as if the strength of her present image with its certainty and righteousness had blotted out the past.

Today, she was a serious woman. He would have called her phlegmatic, except that such a word seemed to deny her physical

14

qualities – the light and grace of her movements, the musicality and gentleness of her voice. But she showed little emotion, she was unmoved by the turmoil around her, by disaster, chaos or success. She presented a calm face, a brow unruffled by Lou's unruliness and Charlotte's rudeness.

Robert believed that her tolerance towards Charlotte might be a result of her relationship with her own mother. Only when she talked of her childhood did her face relax, her smile lose its brittleness. She talked of sunlit days, of mother and daughter in white dresses, sitting together on a swing, walking arm in arm along country roads.

When Lou was younger she would ask, 'Where, Mummy, where did you used to live when you were a little girl?'

Martina would turn an irritated face towards the child. 'Why must you always interrupt, Louisa? Why don't you just listen? And it doesn't matter where we lived. It's gone now, all gone.'

As if the town or county had been wiped from the face of the earth.

Then the tightness around the mouth would be relaxed as she began again to talk of that seemingly happier world where mother and daughter shared such communion, where such sympathy flowed.

Again, Robert's memory let him down and he could recall his mother-in-law only vaguely. He thought that he had met her maybe half a dozen times, before she died while he was off chasing pictures in the wilds of West Cork. As often happened in the excitement of the chase, he hadn't phoned home nor given Martina a number where he could be reached. When he arrived back the funeral was over. Charlotte had been on holiday in Portugal and Robert had often thought since what a tough time it must have been for Martina, with only tiny Louisa by her side.

As Robert rose to pour himself another whiskey, he heard the area door being wrenched open. He knew from the racket that it must be Louisa.

She was dressed in black from top to toe, her black hair cut to within an inch of her scalp. On her feet she wore what looked like sturdy boy's shoes and from her neck hung a large brass crucifix. Robert thought what a wonderful Hamlet she would have made.

'Hi!' She glared at the whiskey bottle. 'You're killing yourself – I suppose you know that?'

'*Chacun à son goût*.' He smiled at his daughter, feeling how she had lightened his mood just by walking into the room.

'What did you do today?'

'The usual.'

As far as Robert knew this meant lounging around various city streets or parks, depending on the weather. She was what she called 'on the doss', having achieved quite a respectable Leaving Certificate but refusing to consider any further education, 'at least until I get my act together'.

'I don't think that's a very good idea, Louisa.' Martina's tone had been one of mild reasonableness. 'What are you going to do in the mean time? And think how disappointed we'll both be, when you have such ability. Your father's family have always had a great respect for education, as indeed — '

'Rubbish. The Persses were thick squireens who went about murdering innocent animals and who wouldn't know the difference between "Tally-ho" and *Tannhäuser*.'

Good for you, Robert had wanted to say, surprised and delighted by his daughter's show of erudition, but the severity of Martina's face inhibited him. He wished he could think of a tactful way of telling her how wrong-headed she was being. Family piety was the last thing that would make Lou change her mind, nor indeed did it seem a good reason to him for the pursuance of further education.

Now Lou took a sip of her father's whiskey. 'Yuk! Is she in?'

'Your mother has not come home yet.' He heard the echo of Martina in his stilted words.

'Then tell her I won't be in to eat – I'm having a pizza in town.'

'Lou — '

But she was gone.

Another night on their own; another dinner *à deux* with the

16

formally set table between them and the straightness of Martina's spine and the slow regularity of her mastication sparking the air with tension. He would clear his throat, she would sip her water; the sound of fork scraping against plate would seem to echo around the kitchen. By the time the meal was over, he would be twitching out of his seat, unable to spend another minute there, craving to be back in his study with his whiskey.

And yet he loved Martina. Or was it love that kept him so alert, so uneasy on her behalf, although for no apparent reason? When he was away from home, he always had a premonition that something awful was happening, that things would have got out of hand by the time he returned. Even when Louisa was only ten, he would say as he kissed her goodbye, 'Look after Mummy for me,' feeling in some fashion Louisa was the more capable.

Then he would return to a shining, ordered house, a wife standing on the steps, smilingly welcoming him back. What was I worrying about? he'd ask himself. What horror did I really expect to find?

He was on his third glass of whiskey when Martina tapped on his door. Her face tightened, then relaxed into an unconvincing smile. 'What a good idea – I think I'll join you. Is there any vodka?'

Robert had learned to live on the surface of life. Most of the time he didn't really hear what Martina said, certainly never to the extent that he noticed her phrasing or the tone in which she spoke. But today he had drunk too much whiskey too quickly; he had spent too much time dwelling on the past, dragging out a tatty store of might-have-beens and stretching them up to be examined in the strong sunlight of noon.

Now, when Martina walked in, he forgot for a moment the reality of his world, foolishly re-starting the struggle which he had lost as a fitter man.

'You don't want a drink, Martina.' He was surprised by the uncontrolled loudness of his voice. 'You don't have to humour me – I'm not an alcoholic or a madman. I won't start chasing you round the house with a breadknife if you don't join me in a drink.'

Martina's pretty laugh was humourless. 'You are a wag, Robert.'

'For God's sake, Martina – stop it. Nobody uses that word. You got it out of some book, like all the rest of your nonsense. What's wrong with us? Surely after twenty years together we can relax, act naturally? Tell me, Martina, what is it?'

Her face was as smooth and expressionless as a doll's; her eyes were opaque blue glass. 'Poor Robert – I can see you've had a hard day. I wouldn't be surprised if you've been overdoing it again.'

Robert sighed. 'Yes, sorry – I didn't mean to sound so grumpy.' Wearily he realized what he had known this morning, that it was futile to struggle against Martina's sustained and fictitious view of things: she was happy, he was happy, and Louisa was a perfect daughter. There were no problems on the horizon, as Robert well knew and admitted except when he was suffering from executive stress, at which time he had to be handled with care. He offered her a smile. 'And you're right – I *am* drinking too much. Here, I'll leave this till after dinner. By the way, Lou's dining in town in some pizzeria. She sends her apologies.' Living with Martina, one ended up talking like a public meeting – anything else seemed too intimate.

'It's probably just as well. Freda's coming round afterwards and you know how they simply don't get on.'

As if anyone could get on with Freda, her harsh strident tones, her dogmatism. Martina's business partner was a big, handsome woman with a large mouthful of improbably perfect teeth. Robert spent the time in her company by silently adding up the cost of the caps that she so prominently displayed. She fascinated him as some spiders did, but Martina would tolerate no criticism of her when he and Louisa fell to giggling about her.

'Unkind,' proclaimed Martina who did not make distinctions between people; and father and daughter looked at one another, shamefaced but resentful.

Robert wondered if part of his wife's oddness was due to her lack of any sense of the ridiculous. Her vision of the world was

depressingly straight, her attitude to others one of kindly tolerance. Far from the madding crowd, that was the impression she
gave – above it all, beyond the fray. And Robert, looking across
the darkening space between them, found his heart wrenched
again by her beauty. Twilight suited her, countervailing her
lack of colour, showing up the perfection of line and bone.
For a woman of such energy she seemed without vitality, the
antithesis of her daughter who, though a lazy little devil, gave
the impression of great bustle. All Martina's movements seemed
languid: you wondered if her hand would ever reach her throat;
her sighs seemed to stop or peter out before they were quite
expelled. It was difficult to believe that she did so much, that
her moments of repose were few, mere brief tableaux interspersed
amidst all the activity.

Martina was looking at her husband but she was thinking of the
past. Almost twenty years since she had married this stranger,
this smiling man. Twenty years – longer than Louisa's entire
life and Louisa was already grown up.

And I am middle aged.

When did one stop feeling like a girl? Never? Charlotte obviously still thought of herself as a great beauty to whom homage
should be paid. Her two mannish daughters also demanded
homage and they had never even been passable. Thick ankles,
large noses, arrogant jaws. Wonderful noses for looking down,
though; all the Persses had them, even Lou, who was pretty as
a kitten.

Martina pondered how similar features differently arranged
could produce such various effects. There was among the Persses
a strong family resemblance. They were of a type, tall and
dark with strongly marked eyebrows and faces where flesh
was subservient to bone. The noses were long and straight,
the chins square. The least notable feature in each face was
the eyes, which seemed surprisingly mild in the midst of all
that authoritative bone.

Yet despite these common features the end results were quite

19

different. The sisters were alike and, if there had been a copper tinge to their complexions, more than anything else they would have reminded one of Indian braves. This was true also of Robert, but in his case the resemblance accorded happily with his gender and most people considered him to be handsome. Louisa's features were a scaled-down, more delicate version of her aunts', and thus missed oddness and achieved prettiness. Martina thought that Charlotte might have shared this if arrogance and hauteur had not added a good two inches to an already long face.

Lou was pretty but, more importantly, she was self-assured. She would demand her place in the sun; Martina had seen to that. It had not been easy, they had both suffered pain. Even now, recalling all those tearful scenes, she recognized the dull and heavy despair that settled in the pit of her stomach. It was the feeling she had had as she turned her back on the piteous little face, walked away from the cries of 'Mummy, don't leave me'. She would grope her way from the birthday party or dancing class, blinded by tears, talking aloud to herself like some mad woman. 'It is good for her, it will make her independent. She may suffer a little now but she will grow up needing no one. Her back will be straight and her heart will be light and she won't even know how to cringe.'

Martina sighed and tried to shake off the burden of loss which always began to gather when she thought of Louisa. The girl was a success, that was what she must concentrate on; she was the one who mattered, not her foolish mother, weighed down now with her soft and selfish thoughts.

Louisa looked the world in the eye and did not find herself wanting. What she would become was irrelevant, Martina knew – she was already a success. She would cope; she would be the one to walk away. Martina need have no fears for her child.

'Let's eat out tonight – how about it, Martina?' Robert was thinking of a cosy restaurant with chatter and cigarette smoke, where the tablecloths were less than pristine and steam rose from the kitchen.

'But everything is ready, the potatoes are almost cooked.'

With a surreptitious slurp from the whiskey glass, Robert followed his wife to the kitchen where cutlery shone and there were flowers on the table. The chill in the air might well have been inside his own head.

3

Louisa kicked her way through the fallen leaves. She was cross, a feeling which commonly assailed her when she approached her home. 'Hi,' she said, passing a group of prostitutes who were already gathering outside one of the darkened houses. She was on nodding acquaintance with many of the girls; they recognized her comings and goings along the deserted square. By six o'clock most of the tall houses were empty, as offices shut up and cars drove off to the suburbs.

Louisa wasn't bothered by the tarts. She even found their presence reassuring, coming home on winter nights. As for their clients who purred around the square in quiet motor cars, they made no mistake with Louisa, her chin held high, her stride unambiguous.

She did, however, hate her house: gloomy and cold and too bloody big.

They had no reason to live there, shivering and miserable inside, surrounded by decay and dirt, but they stayed on because of Martina's delusions of grandeur.

Louisa felt her face grow hot, blood vessels distending as she thought of her mother. Stupid, stubborn, affected, cold . . . most of all, cold. Maybe that was why she didn't notice the temperature inside that ice box – while everybody else was freezing, her reptilian blood told her that it was warm.

Self-pity engulfed Louisa as she stooped to remove some leaves from the sole of her shoe. She thought of the lives of her friends, the cheerful muddle in which they lived. She recalled their untidy kitchens and shabby living-rooms and mothers with badly dyed hair who made you welcome and told you to call again. A nice semi-detached must be heaven, in some friendly suburb where children, not prostitutes, crowded the pavements.

Not that she cared – she'd show them. And he was just as bad. He wasn't really like her but he was weak. He was afraid to stand up to her and tell her to cut the crap once and for all.

Who needed parents, anyway? You didn't choose them and you were stuck with them for a certain number of years, but after that you were on your own. Oh, they'd be surprised, all right, one of these days. They had already written her off without even bothering to find out what she was up to. They left her to do her own thing, accepting any old excuse for absences from home. Just as well she had friends that she could depend on, to whom she could go for encouragement and support.

One of these days, soon, she would walk away. No problem. She would walk away and they would be sorry, or, if they weren't, she wouldn't be there to find out.

'Mother,' she shouted, banging the door after her and clattering up the stairs. 'Mother, where are you?'

Martina sat by a lamp, sewing. She took off her glasses now and looked up at her daughter. 'Do you want me, darling?'

'I've had it with this house. Mother, you don't seem to realize what I have to go through. Dad,' she appealed to Robert who had just come in, 'tell her it's not fair. I have to pass by those girls every single night. It's not very nice for me – is it? I don't think it's very safe even.'

'I'm sure it's quite safe, darling, but I agree, it's not very nice. I don't know why the police don't do something – goodness knows, we've complained often enough.'

'We've been discussing a little car for you, haven't we, Martina? Then you could come in by the mews and you need never see them.'

'I don't want a car,' Louisa bellowed like a baby bull. 'I hate this house. It's far too big for the three of us and it's so spooky at night. I don't know why you want to live here, Mother; nobody else does except for a few old ladies who have nowhere else to go and those loopy Americans.'

In spring and summer the life of the square was augmented by the presence of visiting American scholars who wrote books and finished theses under the grey slates, looking down on the crumbling city. In winter landlords found it hard to rent these garrets.

Louisa, Martina noted with a smile, was a true Persse in her xenophobia. 'It's a beautiful house, darling; can't you see that? I can think of dozens of people who envy us this house. And look how long it's been in the family.'

'Don't start all that again.'

'Besides, you're growing up, Louisa; you'll soon be leaving home. Then you can suit yourself, darling, find yourself something modern and bright.'

'Anyway, Daddy hates it too, don't you, Daddy?' Louisa, changing her ground, was outraged by the suggestion that she was ready to leave the nest. How could you win with a mother like that, who had no decent feelings and who made the sort of suggestions that should properly come from you?

She couldn't now remember why she had wanted to pick a fight with her mother but that didn't matter. Her real grievance against Martina was constant, and constantly reinforced by the sort of remark which now left her fighting back tears. If only Martina would rant occasionally, lay down the law as other mothers did. Then Louisa might be able to believe that she had some feeling for her. 'I can get out now if that's what you want. No problem.'

'Louisa!' Her parents' voices mingled in their joint appeal.

'Come on, Lou.' Robert extended an arm. 'Let's go down to the kitchen and make a cup of tea. We could all do with one.'

'Daddy.' She ran to him and arm in arm they left the room.

Martina replaced her glasses and bent her head once more over her sewing. In the light of the lamp her pale hair had been burnished a luminous gold. As the shadows gathered round her she seemed, in her stillness, more phantom than flesh and blood.

She sighed and it seemed as if the sigh were taken up by the room and settled in sad corners. The shadows moved in a whimper of wind, then stillness and silence returned once more.

In the kitchen Louisa turned on the radio. 'You do hate this place, don't you, Dad?'

Robert offered her a biscuit. 'Of course I do. It's a ghastly barracks of a place, but your mother loves it. It means something special to her – you know that, Lou. Anyway, what a chancer you are, going on about the girls – I know for a fact you're quite pally with them.'

'It's her pretensions that drive me wild, going on all the time about Georgian Dublin. We live in the red light district.'

'Same thing in this town.'

'Wouldn't you just love a nice little flat, or even a house like Granny's?'

'Be kind to an old man, Lou; don't remind me of all those damn steps.'

'I think she's cracked, I really do, Daddy. I mean she's making lots of money, herself and Freda ripping people off, and she won't even heat this place properly. And do you know what she told me? She said that she thinks *en suite* bathrooms are vulgar – I ask you. So I have to go down a flight of stairs just to go to the loo. Cracked.' Louisa's perfect teeth, on whose appearance Martina had lavished so much attention and money, snapped shut on a biscuit, showering crumbs on the tray in front of her.

Robert smiled at his daughter but his heart had been touched by fear. Cracked – the word was so apposite: flawed, damaged. Wasn't that true of Martina, despite her competence and apparent calm?

By marriage to him?

But he was not a bad husband, surely; he didn't beat her up or wage psychological warfare against her. No . . .

He plonked the tea-cosy on the pot. He was getting fanciful. A more likely explanation was that they were all being destabilized by the amount of lead they ingested from the cars that churned past their house all day long. They would all three end up cracked – like the ancient Romans.

He took up the tray. 'Here's a good reason to leave this house, Lou, much more serious than the presence of the ladies outside. The fall of the House of Persse is imminent unless we make a quick move.'

'That's the first good reason I've heard for staying.'

Their laughter preceded them up the stairs, warning Martina who sat, work suspended, looking out at the black face of the night garden.

The house shifted in a sudden gust of wind. Louisa, who was standing at her bedroom window, shivered. The city outside might have been a city of the dead, so totally deserted did the houses around seem. No light showed anywhere, although it was not much after eleven.

At the end of the garden an office block loomed, blotting out Venus and the harvest moon. Louisa often stood and stared at this ugly building which offered irrefutable evidence of the futility of Martina's view of the world. Georgian Dublin was gone, dead, *finito*. Except for tourists and loonies like Martina who could not see the wood for the romance in their eyes.

Seeing her mother as some species of fool helped Louisa to cope; it stopped the awful yearning, the loneliness which often swamped her as she wandered round this large gloomy house. It helped her to shrug her shoulders – nothing she could do about it, anyway – and made escape seem desirable. It also left a loophole which allowed for the possibility of pity rather than hatred dribbling towards Martina.

Louisa jumped as the telephone rang. It was a very loud ring, its decibels having been deliberately raised above normal pitch so that it might be heard throughout the house. As it stopped abruptly, Louisa realized that her parents must still be awake.

Did they ever sleep? Did they, perhaps, when the oak door had closed behind them and they lay down side by side, did they continue with those strange polite conversations, their eyes never quite meeting?

And did they still make love? She found herself blushing in the dark. Her poor father. Louisa knew all about the sex drive of the male, even in somebody as old as Robert. She couldn't imagine him having an easy time with the ice matron. She giggled at this, relieved that she could concentrate on the verbal joke rather than the embarrassment of her parents' sex-life.

'Lou.'

She turned towards the door. Robert stood there, his hair sticking up, his dressing gown falling from his shoulders.

'It's Grandma, Lou.'

'Is she — ' Louisa could suddenly hear her heart pounding in her ear.

'She's had a heart attack. Luckily, she wasn't alone at the time.'

'Where?'

'Playing bridge. Her friends called an ambulance straight away and she's in hospital. We're going in now. You can stay if you — '

'I'm coming.' Anything, rather than stay here in this deserted corner of the world. You could die here . . .

'She won't die, Daddy, will she?'

'We must take it as it comes. Remember she's eighty-four, Lou. Now hurry up and get dressed, there's a good girl. We don't want to delay.'

The porter opened the heavy double doors to them. 'You can wait here. Sister will be over in a minute.' His words echoed in the flagstone passage.

'That means she's dead.' Louisa began to wail.

As Robert put an arm round his daughter's shoulder, Martina turned to look at the inner courtyard. It was dark, its centre quite black where the dim lights from the cloisters did not reach. The walls of the hospital rose all around. The lights from the wards shone yellow and dull. The silence was unnerving, pressing densely down on them.

The tap-tap of footsteps broke into it and they listened to them draw nearer. When Sister appeared out of the gloom it was hard to connect her cheerful face with that disembodied sound.

'The son? And the little granddaughter – isn't that nice! Her friends said they'd contact you when they left the message. Well, poor Mrs Persse has been in the wars, I won't deny that, but she's putting up a great fight. The doctors are working on her now. The heart . . .' Her tone dropped in pitch. 'It actually did stop but they've got it going again. You can go in and see her for a minute soon . . . as soon as the doctors are finished. Now – a nice cup of tea – a nice cup of warm tea?'

They sat outside the coronary care ward, trying to block the sounds that reached them from inside. The nurses coming in and out avoided their eyes, except when they stopped to ask if they'd like more tea.

The assistant matron paused on her rounds to have a chat with them. A very quiet night – they had no idea. Sometimes it could be bedlam in here, particularly at the weekend. Was that tea hot enough? Good.

Martina looked at her watch, then shook it. Twenty minutes. Still, Charlotte was hanging on.

The doctor seemed about Louisa's age, or younger. 'She's put up a remarkable fight.'

'She's — ' Robert stood up.

'She's stable at the moment, the heart is going again. The problem is, at that age, they often get another heart attack, even a series. However . . . Would you like to go in and see her? Sit with her if you like. Be prepared for the tubes and machines, though – she's all wired up. Sometimes the relatives find it upsetting. And talk to her. Hearing is the last sense to go.'

They drove back through deserted streets as dawn was streaking the sky. They had watched by Charlotte's bed, held her hand, talked to her, listened to the queer snorting sounds that came out of her open mouth. At around six o'clock, when the hospital was just beginning to crank into day, a little nurse advised them to go home. 'You'll be exhausted. I know what happens to the relatives – they wear themselves out in the early stage. Go home and get something to eat and some sleep. We'll ring you the minute there's any sign of change.'

They shivered inside the car.

'Can't you get the heat going, Dad? I don't think I ever felt so cold in my life.'

Robert drove through a red light, then was surprised to find himself confronted by a small, black car pawing the ground. Its driver gave him the fingers and, turning down his window, shouted something.

'What did he say?'

'He called you a capitalist swine.'

'More a road hog, surely?'

They laughed nervously, glad of the break in the tension. Louisa twiddled the radio dial but could get only static.

In the back of the car, Martina yawned and thought about strong, hot coffee. The tea had been ghastly, tasting stewed, although it had been freshly made in front of their eyes by Sister. Perhaps it was the water, lying there forever in those vats, occasionally being topped up with disinfectant, just in case.

Cross infection – that's what killed you in hospital. Hazardous places at the best of times and difficult to get out of. Especially if you were wheeled in, toes in the air, like Charlotte.

Beside the car loped Night, a black panther. Robert concentrated on his driving but his ears were full of those awful sounds. They were the sort of sounds that might have been made by creatures struggling to emerge from the primeval slime – sucking, snorting. Not human. Yet issued by the open mouth of his mother.

Oh, the bravery of man, the heroism of his nature. Robert stopped the car, needing to share his love, to express his admiration for his puny species.

He extended a hand to each of his women. 'We'll be all right. We'll be fine. Even if Mother does die, we can cope.'

'Yes, Daddy.' Beside him, Louisa couldn't stop shivering. An abyss had opened up in front of her and she was afraid. She stared into it and wondered about death, what it meant. The absence of Charlotte?

And those awful things she had said – she shouldn't have – she hadn't really meant . . .

She leant backwards, pressing her head into the seat-rest.

Martina dropped a hand on her daughter's head, a surprising and gentle caress.

'I think we should have a good, big breakfast.'

'I agree, Mum. Is there any bacon?'

'I don't think so but I've got some smoked haddock. Anyone fancy some kedgeree?'

The sun had reached the square by the time they arrived home. They stood for a moment on the shallow steps, dazedly looking around them. For once the air was fresh; in the morning light the granite steps glinted. Opposite, a group of evergreens seemed rooted for a thousand years.

Together they raised their faces to the sun before turning to be swallowed up by the dark well of the house.

4

The sisters were in mourning. They had exchanged their usual primary colours for black and it suited them, toning down their aggression and even lending them a degree of chic. They had taken three days off for their mother's funeral, closing the shop in Wicklow where they sold with great vivacity and success the rather lumpy mugs and jugs and candlesticks which they made in their pottery in the back yard. They sat now in Martina's kitchen and discussed the arrangements for Charlotte's funeral as if it were going to be the social event of the year.

It wasn't that they didn't mourn her passing; they did, but they had oodles of common sense. They realized that the time had come and that she had had a long and useful life. They knew, too, that she would not have approved of any unseemly blubbering. Mother had never been one for sentimentality – you got on with life, making the best of it. You had a little weep, blew your nose and got on with it. Anything else was excessive and vulgar and not the Persse way of doing things.

Besides, they were very, very busy. For them, there were not enough hours in the day or days in the week. They took their careers seriously. Without being stuffy about it, they acknowledged that there was a creative element in potting which lifted it out of the realm of mere work. They made no great claims for their talents but neither did they deny them. They felt an obligation to use the gifts which God had bestowed on them, to bring their talents to fruition.

Charlotte would have understood this, they knew, for above all it was their creativity which she herself had cherished.

'I never thought this house could be called useful.' Rosamund smiled kindly at Martina. 'But it's certainly coming into its own today. It's a real advantage having a separate dining- and drawing-room – so few people have these days and it means we can divide everyone into two lots – here.' She handed Martina a list. 'These must be fed, so I suppose they go into the dining-room. These only need a drink. There are rather a lot but I'm afraid they all must be asked back to the house.'

'But – how do you know they'll all be there? I mean – you don't invite people to a funeral, they may not all turn up.'

'Martina – it's Mother's funeral. Of course they'll come.' Rosamund shook her head over Martina's obtuseness and Bunny looked up from her correspondence at the note of exasperation in her sister's voice.

Bunny more closely resembled a horse than a rabbit, but the childhood name had stuck and nobody seemed to find it incongruous, least of all its owner.

She stretched her bony arms over her head and yawned. 'I'm exhausted, utterly done in. I'd rather spend a whole day at the wheel than go through what I've gone through today.' It was generally accepted that Bunny's was the artistic fire behind the sisters' successful enterprise. 'And it's not just the trauma, it's the city. It's so noisy and polluted. I think you're wonderful to live in it, Martina.'

Rosamund stood up. 'Come on, Bunny, let's go and get some air in the park, we could both do with some. We'll take Lou with us if we can find her. And we must all have an early night – we want to be on form for tomorrow.'

'Is everything ready for tomorrow?' Robert manoeuvred his way into the kitchen, both arms encircling a case of whiskey. 'There are going to be several hard drinkers coming and I don't want to run out. Have you sorted out those coming back to lunch?'

'Rosamund left me a list.'

'Oh, good. The girls are being terrific, really, aren't they? Bunny remembered to ring up Mollie Browne. She's an ancient

32

friend of Mother's – I thought she was dead years ago.' edged the large box on to the table. 'What are you giving tl tomorrow?'

'Chicken in white wine sauce.'

'That sounds good.'

Martina listened with distaste to the excitement in her hus band's voice; since his sisters' arrival he had been verging on the ebullient. All these Persses – even Louisa had filled the house with their animation, imbuing the funeral rites of this elder member with a significance that left Martina thoroughly irritated. She thought of all the work which had to be suspended as she started on the gargantuan preparation of the funeral baked meats. A touch of salmonella wouldn't go amiss amongst all those unknown and ravening cousins and uncles.

So unused was Martina to indulging in spleen that she suddenly found her mood lightening. When the sisters returned from their walk there she was, smiling serenely as she chopped carrots at the kitchen table.

There were twenty-five guests at the buffet lunch. They smacked their lips and admitted to peckishness, holding out their plates for second helpings.

Charlotte's name was on every lip: her beauty, her vitality, her bohemianism and spirit in an age when convention had ruled the roost.

'Louisa's taking after her.' The mourners turned to look at the girl who sat ignoring them, glowering out the window and listening to her Walkman. 'And she looks like her too – same wonderful carriage.'

'Obviously lots of character there, Robert,' they told her father.

'Mind you, the Persses were never short of character. Look at the girls.'

The girls stood, backs to the fire, talking severely of their careers. Cousins and aunts marvelled at their artistic flair, their business acumen, girls who had been brought up as gentlewomen – Charlotte's girls.

In her own drawing-room Martina found herself largely ignored. It was not that people meant to be rude, it was just that they had so much to talk about, these Persses *en fête*: so many anecdotes to be re-told, so many fond memories to be shared.

This was clearly a celebratory occasion – they had gathered to celebrate Charlotte's long and happy life. No shadows in this room . . . nothing gloomy. Martina suddenly felt the past clutching at her, trying to pull her backwards, as it had so brutally in the church this morning. She found a bottle of wine and began to circulate.

'More wine, Uncle Hubert?'

'Why not, why not.' He extended his glass but shied back, eyeing her uneasily. She could almost see each group relax as she moved on to the next.

She left the bottle on a table and sat down. Opposite, Louisa sat, her chin on her knees, her eyes closed. Martina was pleased by her preoccupation, pleased by the absent face which she now turned on the room. For a while Martina had been worried, particularly on the night that Charlotte had died. It had looked then as if Louisa might crack up. She had sat shivering in the kitchen, talking incoherently, approaching her mother and then turning from her.

Martina had jollied her along, refusing to recognize the appeal in her daughter's eyes, smilingly offering her a cup of tea in a calm voice while pressing her own arms tightly to her sides, though what she had wanted desperately to do was to fling them around her daughter. It was Louisa's future that was at stake, she had reminded herself; she must see this through on her own and she will emerge all the stronger.

Martina had watched the girl pull herself together, watched her raise her chin and snap that appeal from her eyes. She had taken her look of contempt and told herself that she must be happy for her daughter. As she told herself now before getting up to find an ashtray for a tipsy Persse.

'Time we were off.' The sisters linked arms. 'Can we offer anyone a lift? There's oodles of room in the station wagon.'

The life went out of the party then and uncles began, a shade reluctantly, to empty their glasses. 'Time we were off, too. Goodbye, my dear,' they said to Martina, obviously unable to remember her name. 'It's been very jolly – just what Charlotte would have approved of.'

The house was permeated by a variety of smells – cigar, whiskey, cooking. Robert opened windows before going to the kitchen to load the dish washer. He had packed his women off to bed and he expanded now into a tremendous relief that it was all over. Poor Mother, strange to think that she was gone. But she *was* becoming a burden, better that she should go now. And yet, today . . .

It was natural that he would feel nostalgia today, remembering all the good times. She had been an indulgent mother, especially to her only son. If only she and Martina had hit it off better. Her fault, of course . . . Well, perhaps nobody's fault.

It couldn't be easy for mothers to accept strangers into their family and that was what it amounted to. And their preoccupation must not be entirely selfish for they must worry too about their children. Forgetting about the shortcomings of their own marriages they must hope for perfect happiness for them, ignoring the reality that most marriages were makeshift, the disjunction of two people reared apart being largely unalterable. Even between Mother and Father there had been friction and they had both been Persses, the children of first cousins.

Still, blood did count. Roz and Bunny had walked in on Thursday evening and the three of them had slipped back together, tongued and grooved. It wasn't that there was any great affection between them, it was just that the naturalness of his sisters' presence had seemed very restful. Less room for misunderstandings, less need to explain. And the childhood jokes and references that nobody else found funny but which could still make you laugh with nursery abandon.

Robert sighed and poured himself a whiskey. It was impossible to ignore Martina's behaviour this afternoon, to be unaware of

35

the fact that she had offended most of his relations. What's up? he had said to himself as he saw the chill in her smile, the line of her spine which looked as if it would break rather than bend.

'Are you OK, Martina?' he had asked, taking her aside.

'Of course.'

But the expression had been so wounded that he had found himself being rude to his relations, sure that they must have behaved badly in some way to have caused such a reaction in her. Nice old codgers, poor now for the most part and arthritic, glad of a funeral, which meant something decent to eat and drink. So why did she have to raise her eyebrows at their requests for second helpings, to answer so coldly when they asked her how she was, m'dear?

She was so stiff and starchy. And he was so tired of looking out for her, looking after her.

Lou had come over to him after lunch. 'Chin up, Dad. I know you're missing Grandma; so am I. But the worst is over, things will be less grim after today.'

Now why could Martina not have come over to him and squeezed his hand like that? After all, it was his mother's funeral and it could be thought that he was the one in need of support and comfort.

He refilled his glass. Tonight, when there was no longer any question of divided loyalty, he could admit to himself the truth of Charlotte's often repeated comment: 'She's not a proper wife, Robert. I don't deny her virtues but they are not wifely ones. She is not a proper wife.'

And where did that leave them, or at least him? At crisis point? Certainly, at the moment of reappraisal. Charlotte was dead, Louisa would soon be leaving home; there was no need to justify or patch over or make do any longer. This was the moment to pause and reassess, to open oneself to the possibility that the marriage was over.

The prospect seemed suddenly an exciting one. Or maybe that was the whiskey. *Uisce beatha* – water of life. The only life I've been offered for many years, he thought, with an onrush of self-pity.

He put the whiskey glass from him in sudden disgust. This was maudlin – ridiculous over-reaction. Perhaps he was feeling suddenly orphaned and had therefore been the more disappointed in Martina's failure to comfort him. It was hardly reason enough to decide that the marriage was over, though, to think that he could, or even wanted, to do without the presence of that strange woman who lay sleeping now over his head.

He pictured her, lying quietly, breathing shallowly in her untroubled slumber. He would creep in beside her and, drawing himself up into the foetal position, would find some solace in his proximity to her sleeping form, even as he recognized the arm's length at which she kept his spirit.

A marriage – no more nor less.

At first Martina did not know what had woken her. She felt that she had been roughly wrenched from sleep and for some moments she lay stupidly, not quite knowing where she was. Then she heard and realized that this must have been what wakened her – a sort of high-pitched wail. It rose and fell; after an interval of about ten seconds, it came again. Martina knew from the tenseness of Robert's body beside her that he was already awake.

'It's Lou,' he said, jumping from the bed.

Light flushed into the room from the passage outside. Footsteps pounded on the stairs, a door banged overhead. She listened. The wailing seemed to have stopped; she turned over. Robert would be better at offering comfort.

Martina could not remember her own father; Mother it was who slipped out at night to offer reassurance in the terrifying dark, to offer sips of water and give permission for the light to burn until dawn. You slept in a bedroom off Mother's room. You were not encouraged into her bed except when you were really sick. Then, oh, the comfort, the joy of snuggling into that soft back, of outstaring the black face of night, safe in Mother's arms. It was a penance then to have to get up when morning came, so your cough would get worse, the pain in your tummy become more acute, and Mother, smoothing back your hair, would say, 'Well, a day in bed never did anyone any harm.'

'. . . Martina, for God's sake, can't you see she needs you? Answer her, at least.'

Martina blinked as the figure of her daughter came into focus. 'I'm sorry, darling. Did you have a nightmare?'

Two faces turned on her in anger, teeth bared.

'I told you, Daddy, she wasn't even listening. She doesn't give a damn – she never has.' Louisa's wails had turned to sobs.

'Shh, darling, Mummy's waking up.'

'What am I going to do? I'm alone now – there's nobody to love me now that Granny's dead.'

But – hadn't Granny died years ago? Yes, she had. You and Mother had travelled down by bus to the funeral. The bus had taken hours and Mother had been upset in case you wouldn't get there on time. Then you had to sleep in a neighbour's house because there was no room in Granny's. The house had been cold. Mother had given you hot milk the next morning and rubbed your feet and said, 'I'm sorry I had to leave you, pet. I stayed up the night with Granda, he's in a bad way.'

'I hate her. She's never been a proper mother. She's never cared about me. And she doesn't care about you, either, Daddy.'

Martina shook her head, trying to clear it, to make sense of what was going on. She sat up and saw her daughter's face, tiny and pinched in front of her. She put out her arms. 'Louisa, I'm sorry. Come to me, pet, tell me what's wrong.'

She found herself toppling back on to the pillows, knocked sideways as Louisa flung her off.

'Louisa!'

'Leave me.'

Robert threw her a horrified glance before following his daughter out of the room.

Martina swallowed hard. It was silly to feel rejected. A Persse had died; it was their loss. They must comfort one another.

And she could cope. Of course she could. She must just be careful of her thoughts; she must control them more assiduously. Since this afternoon she had been having difficulties; since that moment in the church when a sunbeam had sought her out and she had suddenly found herself remembering. Another cold stone church, another funeral service.

The wilfulness of memory. It could not, apparently, be destroyed any more than it could be summoned. The vividness of that image this afternoon had left her shaking: the aggression of its return.

Martina got out of bed and went in search of sleeping tablets. It was years since she had used them but she knew that she had some, stuck at the back of some drawer, probably.

She began to rummage.

5

It was mid-November and over Ireland winter had settled in. It hung over the island with damp persistency, filling heads with catarrh and hearts with despondency.

Robert sipped his whiskey and stared out the window.

He didn't know why the house felt so different without Louisa, but it did. She had spent little time at home, especially during the last couple of years. Perhaps it was the very unpredictability of her comings and goings that fluttered a draught of life through these sepulchral rooms.

Looking out on the grey area wall, with the rain slanting against it, Robert felt as if he were entombed.

He would go, he would walk away. Martina didn't need him; that he had ever thought she had seemed ridiculous now. Anyway, he didn't much care any more; he had hardened his heart against her. Her reaction to Louisa's departure had shocked him, leaving him gaping at her incredulously.

'Probably for the best.'

'But – didn't you hear what I said? She's gone – Lou is gone. She's just walked out, here's the note. She says she's going to London. What will she live on?'

'Has she taken her bank book?'

'Martina – she's only nineteen.'

Martina had put down her sewing and stood up. She had walked across to where he was standing and, putting her arms around him, she had kissed him with cold, dry lips. 'You really must not worry, Robert; Louisa can look after herself. I brought her up to be independent and I assure you – she'll be fine.

Anyway, I think it's a good thing for young people to get away from home. She can always come back when she's spread her wings a bit.'

Then she had resumed her seat. The subject was closed.

As Robert watched her during the following days, he noticed an appetite undiminished, a sleep pattern undisturbed. Her hand was steady, her smile serene. In bed, she was as desirous of him as ever and his humiliation was complete when, for the first time since they married, he found himself unable to respond, limp and indifferent to her clever hands.

Calmly, Martina had put on her nightdress. 'I'll go and find something that will help me get to sleep.'

So that's what he had been supplying all those years – a soporific. Then she had better look to her chemical alternative.

Turning his back on the rain, he poured himself another drink. He would leave the house to Martina; it would be unfair to turn her out when it meant so much to her. He would find himself an attic somewhere; he could even kip in the gallery if the worst came to the worst. He could see himself in a sleeping bag on the floor, surrounded by all those mediocre pictures. Perhaps he could come home for a bath occasionally, although as the deserting husband he might find doors barred, locks changed.

The telephone bell rescued him from this dreariness.

'Is that Mr Persse?'

'Speaking.'

'Isn't that lucky, now. I took the chance of looking up the book – it *is* Mr Robert Persse?'

'Who is this?'

'Tom Egan, Mr Persse.'

'Who?'

'No, you wouldn't remember me – how could you? The cemetery, Mr Persse, Mount Allen. I'm the caretaker there. We had a bit of a chat after the funeral, if you remember.'

'Of course, yes. What can I do for you, Mr Egan?'

'Are you sitting, sir? This is going to come as something of a shock. It did to me and that's why I hesitated, not wanting to upset you. But the Board met and I had to tell them and they said that I was obliged — '

'I think you'd better just tell me, Mr Egan.'

'Well . . .'

Robert threw the bit of black plastic from him and backed away from it as if he had been holding a large tarantula instead of a piece of harmless and useful technology. Then he replaced it properly, cutting off the voice which squawked, 'Are you there still, Mr Persse? Are you, sir?' But fearing that the man might ring again, he plucked it up and threw it once more on the desk.

He had to have time to think . . . but he mustn't think. Images kept crowding on to his retinae, hurtling along at the wrong speed. He took up his glass but gagged as the whiskey flooded his mouth.

Maybe there was some mistake; maybe old Egan had finally flipped his lid after years of living among the dead. No – the voice had sounded steady, sympathetic; the description and the details –

No, he couldn't allow himself to think about it. He must give himself time, prepare himself. And he was filthy, he had begun to smell . . . He had to wash, to clean himself. Then he might begin to think about it, but not till then.

Returning home, Martina found lights on everywhere but no sign of her husband. 'Robert?' she called, walking along the passage to the study. She sniffed the air, then noticed the overturned glass on the rug. The best part of a glass of whiskey, she guessed, from the dimensions of the dark stain.

'Robert?' she called again, this time running towards the stairs.

It was only when she found his clothes strewn on the bedroom floor that she thought of the bathroom.

'Are you all right?' She tapped on the door. Surely he had had a bath this morning?

'Yes,' the answer came after a pause. 'Don't make me anything to eat, though. My stomach's a bit queasy.'

She was shocked by his appearance when he did eventually come down.

Despite the bath he looked dishevelled, red-eyed and bloody from several shaving nicks around his chin. Martina tried to keep her eyes away from the whiskey glass in his hand.

'How are you feeling now?'

'OK.' The voice trembled upwards, out of control on the second syllable.

'Robert. At least sit down.'

Ignoring her advice, he began to move around the kitchen, putting his hand out to ward off sharp edges, as if it were the doors and chairs that were moving.

'Martina.' She turned from the oven at the appeal in his voice. 'Martina – it's Mother's grave.'

'What?'

Leaving the oven she walked to the window to look out on the still falling rain.

'I find it difficult even to put it into words, it's so – so unimaginable.' He lowered his head, staring into his glass. 'It happened on the day after the funeral – no, the day after that, as far as the caretaker knows. He was going past the grave and he saw – he saw that somebody had shat on it.'

Robert took another gulp of whiskey and another prowl round the room.

'He thought that it must have been some child that got in when he wasn't looking, but then it happened a second time. At first he wasn't going to tell me because he knew how upsetting it would be, but then he began to get upset himself and to wonder and imagine why it had happened. So he phoned me today and told me. I don't know – it's just that I can't make sense of it. I keep on seeing the grave and . . . You won't believe this, Martina, but it's somehow worse than her death.'

'Oh I do, I do.' She blinked as light from a passing car illuminated the area, silvering the slanting rain as it fell. 'There are worse things than death; I know that, Robert.'

'And it's strange how much I miss her – I didn't think I

would. She was such an awful woman in so many ways. But there's just this great sense of loss, of emptiness. I keep on thinking of things I want to ask her about and then I realize all over again that she's gone.'

'She's your mother, Robert, it's only natural.'

'But this – there's nothing natural about this. It's so sick, so malevolent. That's what makes it so awful. I mean, why would anybody want to do such a thing?'

'Don't think about it any more.'

'I can't help it. I can't get it out of my head, away from my eyes. Why would they do it? Against the dead? She was a silly woman but she never harmed anyone. It's because it doesn't make sense: that's what's so awful. The senseless hatred of such an act.'

'Maybe it was just accidental.'

'Twice? No – deliberate hatred.' He began to shiver so that the glass knocked against his teeth. 'I'm afraid, Martina, afraid that there's something out there waiting to get me. Look what's happened: first Mother's death, then Lou's disappearance . . . now this. Everything's beginning to disintegrate. I can't – Martina, help me.'

She turned and took him in her arms, patting his back, smoothing down his hair where it stuck up around the crown.

'You mustn't worry any more; I'll look after you. Come on, I'm putting you to bed. And you've had enough whiskey.'

Taking him by the hand, she led him from the kitchen.

An air of calm possessed the bedroom with the curtains drawn against the night and the light from the lamps suffused and rosy. Underneath his blankets Robert was tranquil and secure. He had been fed scrambled eggs by Martina, and toast which she had cut up into tiny triangles before popping them into his mouth. Now she lay by his side, her breath gentle on the back of his neck. It was years since he had felt so cosseted.

It wasn't that he had forgotten his sorrows – the loss of Lou, the desecration of his mother's grave – but over the last few hours he had gained some strength. With Martina beside him

44

he felt that he could face up to things, and the knowledge that she was with him made the world a less threatening place.

Martina had changed: from the moment that she had put her arms round him in the kitchen, he had felt a radical shift in their relationship. Now he was leaning on her and sure that she could support him. He had been surprised by her kindness and then surprised by his surprise. Had it been kindness, then, which had been lacking, which she had refused to give? Not always, surely?

There was something familiar about the feeling in his body, the ease spreading through his limbs, the lightness around his heart. In contrast, Martina's presence, her spirit, tonight was somehow different. It was a presence which corresponded to or perhaps evoked his sense of ease and it began to summon forth tantalizingly another figure – a pliant girlish figure that lay beside him breathing quietly, the pores of whose skin exuded love.

That was it – but what? He sat up suddenly, trying to make sense of his discovery.

That Martina had stopped loving him or withheld her love and that only tonight had that love begun to flow again?

Surely a fanciful and extravagant deduction, and yet he knew it to be true. Emotions did not have to be put into words to be understood. They attacked the heart before they ever reached the head. Maybe that was why he had been so slow to recognize what now seemed so obvious. And maybe his head had always lagged behind his heart, dawdling fearfully. At any rate, tonight it was working, and, as it marshalled the facts, a pattern of behaviour began to make sense. For many years now there had been no peace in this room or bed. Passion, yes, but that passion had been fuelled by hostility; suddenly he was sure of that. No wonder he had lain awake as Martina had slumbered by his side, for it was while she slept that her silent aggression towards him was at its most potent, oozing out over him, unfiltered by speech.

He lay back on his pillows, dizzy with his new insight. It was too novel to cause him any unhappiness, and it explained so much. As to why she had harboured such resentment or why it had evaporated so suddenly he didn't know, and he wasn't so sure that he wanted to. He stretched out a hand and felt the soft and loving contours of the body beside him. Something had been released in her tonight, some hard constriction had snapped. Martina was as she had been once upon a time, a loving and tender presence. Recognizing now the absence of her ill-will, he wondered how he had lived with it all these years without seeing it for what it was.

Poor Mother. Perhaps some good had come after all from that act of desecration. And perhaps that horrid act had not been personal in any way, just the random exercise of some sick soul, choosing the grave because of its newness or its proximity to a path.

Tomorrow he must try to make reparation. He must rake the soil, strew it with flowers. He must buy flowers, too, for the living in his life. He was not a man of gestures but he could always change. There could be a new beginning for Martina and himself.

As he fell asleep, he had a final perception. Ruefully he realized that their passionate love-life was probably a thing of the past. He did not know why this should happen but instinctively he knew that it would.

Next morning he opened his eyes reluctantly. The unsympathetic morning air told him that his imaginings of last night had been no more than that. Then Martina came in with the breakfast tray and smiled at him and he thought: Everything is going to be all right.

'I knew things were looking up,' she said. 'I felt it in my bones last night. Look – what have you got to say about this?'

It was a postcard from Louisa. 'I've got myself a job as a chambermaid in a posh hotel. I won't tell you where as I don't want you to come and get me. Anyway, don't worry, I'm fine. Just getting my act together.'

They stared at the shiny picture of Tower Bridge, Martina making no comment, merely squeezing Robert's hand.

'You were right,' Robert acknowledged. 'I should have known you were. Louisa will be fine.'

46

'I think she will, and I think you should stay in bed for the day.'

'I'm not sick.'

'You need a rest; besides, there are certain things I want to discuss with you. Leave the gallery for one day and settle back. I'll get us some more coffee.'

There was an unaccustomed, almost mischievous gleam in her eye as she left the room, reminding Robert suddenly of Louisa.

When she had poured out the coffee and sat down in a chair facing the bed, she seemed overcome by shyness, picking at her nails, clearing her throat, seemingly finding it difficult to begin her discussion.

'Well, Martina? What's so momentous?'

'I've been thinking. In fact, I thought quite a lot last night . . .'

'And?'

'Robert – why don't we change our lives completely? Louisa's going made me think about it, and then – last night. We could sell this house – what you and Lou have wanted for years. I could give up my business; Freda would find someone else. You could close down the gallery, at least temporarily. We'd be free, Robert! We could do what we liked – travel, see the world before we're too old.'

The heady concept of freedom filled the air between them. They smiled across at one another tentatively, fearful of causing it damage in any way.

'We could travel on the Orient Express.'

'The Trans-Siberian Railway. We could visit Vladivostok.'

'Arkhangel.'

'Valparaiso.'

'El Dorado.'

'I don't know why I didn't think of it years ago. Have you any idea what these houses sell for?'

'But you love this house, Martina.'

'One can outgrow love.'

If Robert imagined that Martina had been indulging in harmless fantasy, he was brought up sharp that evening when she returned to the bedroom with a whiskey for him and the news that the house was now with an auctioneer, date of auction to be arranged, and that her business partnership with Freda had been dissolved.

'Isn't that all rather rushed?'

'What's the point in delaying? I've thought about it and I've made up my mind – I thought we both had.'

'Yes.'

But he was filled with fear for her. What would she do without her work, without her house? She would be like a snail without its shell, creeping around the streets of Dublin, leaving a silvery trail of broken-down defences behind her.

The house meant more to her, he would have said, than anything else in her life, and that included her husband and daughter. She had thrown it the sort of looks she had never thrown them, had walked up and down its staircases caressing it, rubbing against its walls and panelling as a cat did around one's ankles when it wanted food.

And now she was disposing of it without a backward glance.

'Where will we live?'

'We can buy a little house further out of town. I had thought about a flat but I would miss a garden. And small houses are cheaper, anyway, than flats.'

Her face glowed, her usually pale cheeks stained a faint pink. Robert realized that he knew her less well now than he had, or thought he had, when they got married. She was uncharted country and very desirable.

That night they made love. He took the initiative, aware, even in his enjoyment, of a new passivity in Martina. Afterwards, he felt a small pool of dismay gather with the ridiculous notion that he had defiled her.

A queer interlude now began for them. They were gentle with one another, as if they were both invalids recovering from long illnesses. Like invalids, they spent their days pottering, lingering over meals, talking desultorily of their future.

Martina was already withdrawing herself from the house,

spending more time with Robert in the basement. He would be glad to be rid of it, to have its listing grey weight off his back. It now seemed to him that it had put a blight on their lives, the very multiplicity of its floors pointing up the separateness of their existences. Martina had lived at a distance in chilly grandeur, whilst he had slunk in the basement, sipping whiskey for warmth and comfort. And the corridors and stairwells had echoed and sighed; the winds had rattled those long, mournful windows and depression had settled over everything.

On occasion he had walked in the garden of the square or sat there on a bench on sunny mornings. There was seldom anyone else around and, as he sat or walked, he was made aware of the unbearable weight of the city crowding down. He listened to the screaming of car engines, the hysterical tap-tapping of high-heeled shoes, and it seemed to him at such moments that the city was occupied by frantic people and that there was no choice between that state and his own lethargic dullness.

They had to escape, rid themselves of all that. If they could live in a road where chaps went off to work in the mornings, where wives gossiped over garden walls and borrowed cups of sugar – if they could live in such a world, it would surely give them access to normality, it would be the touchstone of the blessedly ordinary.

Robert believed that it had been the oddity of the relationship between her parents that had driven Louisa away. He still could not agree with Martina that it was a good thing – Lou was far too young.

Now he no longer put the blame solely on Martina, feeling sure that he was just as culpable. This gentle, even tender creature by his side was nothing new; this was the girl whom he had married and whom he had, however inadvertently, deformed into something else in the intervening years.

He was hopeful now, however – their lives had already changed. And he had recovered from the incident with Charlotte's grave. It had not been repeated and he had come to believe in its accidental rather than malevolent nature. He could put it behind him.

The auctioneer who came to see the house congratulated them

on its careful and loving restoration. 'A gem, a positive gem. It will make money – and I mean money.'

Timidly, they began to discuss the future.

'Any regrets, Martina?'

'None. Except that I should have done it years ago. You and Louisa were right all this time and I couldn't see it.'

'And work?'

'I've sewn enough hems to last me a lifetime.'

Robert had been thinking the same thing about selling pictures, at least the sort of pictures that found their way into his gallery. 'I've decided definitely to close the gallery.'

'Yes – well, you haven't really been enjoying it, have you, for a long time now.'

Not for fifteen years, when he had determined to keep it open to – what? Show the world? Prove his integrity? Win back his good name?

Robert Persse had been a spoilt and amiable young man who had sailed through life, the quintessential dilettante. He came from a family where the habits and expectations of wealth were innate, although there had been no real money around since his grandfather's time. He hadn't thought how to make a living, and halfway through a classics degree (whose utilitarian value was in any case strictly limited) he left Trinity and walked up Kildare Street to enrol in the College of Art. He would be a painter.

Charlotte had applauded his decision. She was a snob, but not a philistine, and she would prefer to see her son a painter than a schoolmaster in some minor English public school which would employ him in preference to someone with a degree from Manchester or Glasgow.

Within months, Robert realized that he would never be a painter, but the instinct which had led him to the art world had not been a false one, for he discovered within himself a real talent – he was a connoisseur. Put him in front of a canvas and his reaction was swift, his judgement assured. This not particularly forceful young man would make pronouncements without hesitation. The strength of his convictions led others to believe that he must know what he was talking about. And he did. He responded to the medium; he derived pleasure from it. Untroubled by fashion, he had a sure eye that spotted real talent as it discarded the bogus, the imitative.

His limitation was that his vision seemed confined to the contemporary. He was ignorant of the history of art, although he would just about have recognized *The Last Supper* or *The Burial of Count Orgaz*. But the work of past centuries did not speak to him, most of the painting in the National Gallery leaving him unmoved. With the fierce energy of the twentieth century, with its stops and starts, its unresolved blocks of passion, he was quite at home.

Towards the end of his second year at college a fellow student turned to him one day and said, 'What you should be doing, Persse, is helping to sell people like me. You'll never make a painter.'

Having come to this conclusion already, Robert was not offended. Indeed, he was excited by this new idea. Suddenly he knew he had found his niche – he would open an art gallery. Charlotte, ever ready to accommodate her son, swallowed her disappointment and set about finding the money to buy the lease on a suitable premises.

Everybody, even Robert himself, was surprised by the success of the gallery. In the mysterious manner of these things, it caught on, and within two years reputations were being made and lost on the strength of Robert Persse's patronage.

When Martina met him, he was riding the air like a young falcon, delighted with the world, full of grace. He was without avarice and largely without ambition. He was doing what he wanted to do, and by some accident he happened to be good at it. He treated his artists well, charging less commission than the other galleries because, if he liked your work, he genuinely thought it a privilege to be allowed to exhibit it. Everyone loved Robert – a golden lad. Charlotte, pleased that the world recognized what she had always known, boasted of his success among her friends and relations. Soon, the owners of windswept, crumbling mansions throughout the counties of Ireland were rooting in attics and disused stables, searching for lost or forgotten treasure that they might leave at the door of Robert's gallery. In the ordinary way, they would have had no truck with dealers, but Robert was one of their own and many of them knew that only the discovery of hidden treasure could at this stage keep the water out and the dry rot down.

Robert wasn't interested in these, for the most part, filthy canvases but he took a selection of the least dog-eared and showed them in a room behind the main gallery.

And he did, inadvertently, have some successes. An early Jack B. Yeats fetched a handsome price for its owners, as did a Roderic O'Connor. Then, one morning, a frail old lady came panting up the stairs of the gallery, followed by a man carrying a large plastic-covered rectangle.

How many times afterwards Robert was to ask himself the question why hadn't he followed his initial reaction, which was to bundle the old lady, taxi driver and picture out the door, before the plastic had been removed? Perhaps because it had all happened so quickly and the man had thrust the painting at him and the old lady had seated herself and was telling her story before he had time to open his mouth.

She had travelled all the way up from Sligo by train, with the canvas resting against her knee. The previous night she had taken it down from its place over the drawing-room mantelpiece, where it had hung as long as she could remember. It was a self-portrait by her aunt and she had always been led to believe that it was of some value. Her aunt had been as talented as she was beautiful, an intimate friend of Sarah Purser. The portrait was somewhat discoloured because of the smoke, but wasn't it true that pictures could be successfully cleaned, without damage? It was a wrench to part with it, made easier, however, by the knowledge that Mr Persse would be handling the negotiations.

Robert looked in despair from the black wrapping to the old lady. It was one thing to have on exhibition minor RHA

52

luminaries from the early years of the century, but quite another to give wall-space to the amateur daubings of some gentlewoman. Before he knew where he was, he would be showing samplers.

Then he saw the little face opposite him, the blue eyes beseeching and yet bright with pride. 'I'll be delighted to handle your aunt's portrait and thank you for asking me.' With his sort of success he could afford to be generous.

The picture had been bought by Hubert Moffat while it was still standing in a corner waiting to be cleaned. Perhaps Robert should have been alerted by the price Hubert had offered, but, after all, he had known him at Trinity and he had quite willingly believed his explanation that there was a market for that sort of thing among London *arrivistes* who were indifferent to art but interested in furnishing their walls with the portraits of newly acquired ancestors.

In any case, despite his discovery of the Yeats, Robert was still only interested in the contemporary. Excitement for him lay in the recognition of new talent, in bringing some unknown into his rightful place in the sun. He had barely glanced at the old lady's picture and, when Moffat offered him money, thought only of how pleased she would be to get such a good price.

Two months later, he had been rung up by a reporter from the *Irish Times*. 'Any comment on the sale of the Mancini?'

'The what?'

'It was sold this morning in Christie's. What did Miss Tanham think of the price? Has she been in touch?'

Miss Tanham had been right about most of the details: her aunt had been a talented amateur painter and a renowned beauty; she had moved in artistic circles and been a friend of Sarah Purser; but the portrait of her that had hung over her niece's fireplace had been painted not by her but by Antonio Mancini.

Robert soon discovered that to protest his innocence was to protest too much. When the story was pieced together it seemed incontrovertible that he had deliberately cheated an old and impoverished lady.

His friendship with Moffat pointed towards collusion; more

damning still was the sudden realization of who he was – a Persse, a member of a family already tainted by artistic fraud. Throughout Ireland could be heard the sound of arthritic spines straightening and old disused memories clicking into life as the remnants of the gentry began to make the connection between Sir Hugh Lane and Robert Persse. Lane's mother had been a Persse and clearly it was on that side of the family that the bad blood lay. Nursery or schoolroom memories were refreshed, the comments of one's parents recalled, and for a week or two the Hugh Lane controversy lived again. Nobody was too clear on the details, but that it was or had been shocking was beyond doubt. Something about passing off a copy of a Corot as an original, but, much worse, Lane had tried to dupe the Prince of Wales himself.

Useless to point out to them that Sir Hugh Lane was considered a great benefactor to his country, that one of the two art galleries in Dublin was named after him; useless to point out that, in any case, Robert Persse was only a distant cousin. Anglo-Ireland was having more fun than it had had since the days of viceregal splendour, and it had no intention of allowing such minor details to curtail its enjoyment.

Among the young artists, Robert's friends, who saw the Lane analogy as so much tosh, there was, nevertheless, a readiness to believe that Robert had known what he was doing. Dealers, they knew, even the best of them, were exploiters: that's how they made a crust, ripping someone or other off. And how could anyone believe that a portrait by Mancini had been painted by some slip of a girl without any formal training?

What caused Robert most pain in the whole affair was a letter he received from Miss Tanham telling him that she did not at all believe in his guilt, that if blame was to be laid anywhere it was at the door of her faulty memory and that she was not dismayed at the amount of money she had got. It had enabled her to do a job on the roof and that was all she had ever wanted.

Fifteen years later, Robert still felt a twinge of regret that all that money had found its way into Moffat's greedy fist and had not ended up where it belonged, with Miss Tanham. Otherwise, he did not repine. When he looked at pictures nowadays his enjoyment was all the greater because it was not proprietary. He had never really believed in his own success and, whereas the loss of his good name had worried him, it seemed that the moral climate had changed over the years and to be suspected now of double-dealing was to be admired. Charlotte used to say that this was because their sort were all dying and the natives were now in high places; whatever the reason, the social world was ready, even enthusiastic, to receive Robert should he show any interest in entering.

Robert would close his gallery without a glance back at the past. He would sell this house with pleasure and he would rescue Martina from the shadows she had lived among for too many years. He stretched out a hand towards her and drew his finger along the line of her jaw. 'Come to bed,' he said and, obediently, she rose. As they walked upstairs, hand in hand, Robert realized how changed were his sexual responses. Before, in what now seemed like the distant past, he had waited almost passively for Martina's initiatives and had fully enjoyed them when they came. He had not, however, been excited by his wife; he did not find himself at odd times during the day overwhelmed by sexual desire as he looked at her working in the garden or shoving chops around the pan.

Now that was changed. Since the night she had put him to bed and fed him scrambled eggs, Robert had been aware of a new sexual *frisson*. The air between them crackled with it; their eyes could not meet without admitting to its presence. Robert was like a tumid schoolboy, embarrassed but delighted by his plight.

The corollary of this was strange, for Martina, who aroused such passion in him, had become a much duller sexual partner. She was now the passive one, lying beside him in wifely obedience but with none of her old fire and flair. Her compliance roused him further, filling him with contradictory emotions.

Feeling her hand inside his, he was aware of how easily he

could crush it, crush her, tear her apart. And because of this knowledge he knew that he would be extra gentle, extra careful, and that his love-making would that night have the piquancy of latent sadism. Always latent, never active, because he loved Martina.

6

Bunny phoned Robert at the gallery. 'Now don't talk, just listen, because this is costing me a fortune. We've got Louisa.'

'What do you mean, you've got Louisa?'

'She's come to us. Poor darling, she was afraid to go home, she didn't know how you'd react to her leaving London.'

'Bunny – this is stuff and nonsense. We didn't even want her to go in the first place. Let me speak to her.'

'She doesn't want to and I've promised I won't throw her to the wolves — '

'Bunny!'

'In a manner of speaking. Anyway, I said I'd ask you both to come down and discuss it here on neutral ground. She can stay on here if she likes; we'd be delighted to teach her our craft. Financial arrangements can be worked out later.'

'We'll be down tomorrow, Bunny, tomorrow afternoon. Try to hold on to Lou until then. Tie her up if necessary but don't let her get away until we arrive.'

He was humming as he put down the phone. He hadn't allowed himself to think too much of Louisa; he hadn't admitted to himself how much he had been missing her. He didn't care why she had gone or why she had returned: it was enough to know that she was back. Tomorrow they would bundle her into the back of the car and take her home with them. He was reaching out his hand to phone the news to Martina when he decided to go home early and tell her in person.

57

Martina was standing at the sink, shaking lettuce leaves into a salad spinner.

Taking her hands, he began to dry them on a tea towel. 'I've got news for you.'

'What?' Her eyes shone up at him.

'Lou's home.'

'What? Here?'

'No, she's with the girls – some nonsense about being afraid to face us. You know what a minx she is.'

Martina drew her hands away and sat down. Her face had turned white. 'I don't believe you.'

'Martina – aren't you pleased?'

'I don't believe you – why should she come back – why should she leave London? She's only been there a little over a month. And why should she go to them?'

'Maybe she's come for Christmas – but, does it matter? She's home.'

He could see it did. Martina's hands were trembling, she was shaking her head in reflex action, her eyes glazed. 'She's my daughter – do you think I don't know her? Do you think I didn't rear her? I love her.' Her voice shook with passion. 'But I let her go because I knew she could cope. She wouldn't come slinking back. And to them.'

'But she's coming home to us tomorrow – we're going down to collect her. What is it, Martina? Why are you so upset?'

But she had gone, slamming the door on his words and leaving him to puzzle over her reaction.

By the time he had set the table and finished drying the salad, she was back. Robert took one look at her and felt apprehension cold in his stomach. The old Martina stood in front of him, a perfect resurrection. She emanated purpose and efficiency: her eyes, her limbs, her hair even, seemed charged, as if by an electric current. The timbre of her voice when she spoke had recovered its old cold sparkle. 'I think you should retrieve Louisa, Robert, on your own.'

'Won't you come? She'll want to see you.'

'I think not.' The reply was ambiguous. 'In any case, I'm rather busy tomorrow afternoon.'

'Doing what, for heaven's sake?'

'Please Robert, there's no need to shout. You go and fetch her, although I should be surprised if she'll want to come with you. After all, she passed the door going to Wicklow. But go and see for yourself. I shouldn't bother. She knows where we live.'

That night his insomnia returned while Martina lay on her back in untroubled sleep.

It was as if the intervening weeks had never been and he didn't think he could bear it. He had lived equably enough with the old Martina, but that was before he had known the captivation of the new. Now that she had been whipped away again, he was filled with despair. After Bunny had phoned and before he had gone home, he had begun to plan Christmas. It would be their last Christmas in this house and he determined that they would go out with a bang. He had decided to blow Charlotte's small legacy on a spectacular festival. Throughout the house radiators would gurgle as the thermostat was turned up; lights would blaze from every window; champagne would lie cooling in silver buckets and he and Lou would deck the rooms with greenery.

He was struck by the symbolism of it and filled with a pagan delight. The gods of darkness were beginning a retreat; the old year was dying and with it was going their old life. Their daughter had come home and, reunited in love, they would turn and face towards spring and its long, shadowless days.

Now Martina, in what seemed no more than pique, had destroyed this vision of happiness. He knew that there was no chance of discussion with her; she had already retreated too far for that.

Mad Martina.

The words were out and began whirling around inside his skull.

Lovely Martina, his darling.

Her reaction had been disproportionate, though, to such a degree that surely hinted at the pathological.

He left her and turned his thoughts to himself, to the sterile days and nights which would ensue; to the cold bleak dawns and silences which would well up inside the house so that the air would be swollen with discontent. She might even now decide to keep the house.

If she did that, he would divorce her.

He recalled the sense of liberation which that thought had brought to him before. To be free of all human relationships – a consummation devoutly to be wished but impossible to achieve, he feared, given his dependent nature. He would have said human nature if he hadn't recalled with whom it was he was sharing a bed.

Eventually, he fell asleep, a blank anaesthetizing balm which offered him respite as car doors banged outside in the square and prostitutes, grinding out cigarette butts under their heels, hitched their skirts and sat into cars, wondering when those bloody punters would go home. Christmas week was always the most hectic.

'Well then, Louisa, what's all this nonsense?'

Louisa offered her father a shamefaced smile. 'I thought you'd be pleased to see me.'

'I am, but why didn't you come straight home? And what brought you over there in the first place?'

'Dad – give us a break.'

'No, Louisa – you've behaved like an idiot.'

'Yeah. Well. I suppose she's furious that I'm back. I notice she didn't bother coming down.'

'Don't change the subject.'

'I'm not.' Suddenly she lunged at him and threw her arms around him. 'It's good to see you, Dad.'

He found himself laughing. 'You haven't changed, Lou. Come and sit on my knee. You're looking well.'

'And you.'

Robert wondered how he had ever let her go, how he had lived for so long without her. 'You will come home with me, won't you, Lou?'

He looked around him. The room was furnished with a mixture of modern tat and more solid Victorian furniture. The many lamps had all been thrown on the premises and now leaned crookedly, giving the room a drunken air. On the walls was a profusion of amateurishly executed pictures in different media. The sisters, being potters, moved in artistic circles and had many generous friends.

'What are you doing here, anyway, Lou? I think you're a coward; I think you were afraid to face us and that's why you came sloping down to the girls.'

Louisa glared at her father. 'At any rate, I know I'm welcome here and I should have thought you'd be glad to have me back from London.'

'Your mother and I — '

'Leave her out of it.'

'Lou.'

'She's never had any time for me. She was probably glad to see the back of me. She'd be really happy if I emigrated to Australia.'

Bloody women.

Robert banished this thought and looked at his daughter, shining before him with good health and resentment. She would survive: the firm flesh, bright eyes, lustrous hair; the strong hands and teeth and good firm feet.

The other woman in his life was more fragile. More beautiful, too, he admitted sadly, not quite knowing whether the sadness was for the daughter or for the wife.

'Stay here, darling, if you want to. We're selling the house – I'll let you know as soon as we get somewhere else. We're looking every weekend.'

The momentary gleam of interest was quickly quenched. 'Nothing to do with me.'

'No, but there will always be a room for you, if you want it.'

Robert set out for home in the country-black night. There

were no stars out and, once he had left the village behind, the land through which he travelled seemed uninhabited. His headlamps shone on the wet road surface and a smell of damp vegetation crept into the car. Even the powerful heater failed to dispel the chill.

As he approached the city, he found himself dazzled by a stream of oncoming traffic, commuters cheerfully leaving the city behind. Robert gripped the steering wheel, filled with an anxiety to get home and yet a dread of arriving.

At Kilmacanogue, he stopped at a pub. It wasn't a drink he wanted but the hum of human voices, the reassurance of human contact. But he had a drink, and then another. As he listened to the flow of talk and stared at the coloured lights on the Christmas tree, he felt himself, his world, more threatened.

Nothing had been resolved. There had been a desperation in Louisa's farewell hug so that he felt, in spite of her reassurances, that he was abandoning her. And he could picture Martina's reaction when he arrived without her. She would smile at him, all snap and sparkle, her pathetic attempt at indifference fooling not even herself, he imagined. He didn't blame Louisa; he couldn't blame Martina; that they both blamed him he realized and accepted without understanding why.

He dragged himself out of the pub into the dank evening, and forced himself once more behind the wheel.

The nearer he got to Dublin, the slower he found himself driving, so that approaching the square he had to put on a burst of speed, in case he was mistaken for a client by the prostitutes.

'I'm home,' he called, depressing a switch in the darkened house. In the kitchen there was a note, and a red light showing in the oven. He ladled stew on to a plate, then scraped it into the dustbin. The whiskey had given him a headache and his mouth was dry from the dry heat of the car. He had no appetite – for anything. Martina was probably already asleep, although it was not yet nine o'clock. He wondered what he would do with the rest of the night, wishing he was the sort of man who could join his mates in the pub or fall asleep in front of the television set. He toyed with the idea of walking out on to the front steps and clicking his fingers in the air. Would one of the girls come running? He could let her in by the area door, take her into the study. Martina would not even hear. She would sleep on over their heads, dreaming whatever it was she dreamt about in her tranquil sleeping hours.

He had no desire: without Martina he was emasculated. If she were to leave him now, he could picture himself growing plump and soft, his body hair disappearing, the palms of his hands turning dough-like and sweaty. A eunuch.

At ten o'clock he went to bed, because there was nothing else to do. He lay, his arms folded under his head, staring into the dense and silent dark. Beside him, Martina whimpered, then settled back. He moved away from her towards the edge of the bed. Her body gave off no heat but a cold and malevolent chill. Or so it seemed to Robert.

This was ridiculous, this was black fantasy. What was coming over him? Maybe a simple case of the heebie jeebies – his head giving out before his liver, paranoia rushing in to fill the vacuum left by the receding whiskey. His grandfather, who had fought in the Great War, had often talked of the heebie jeebies, of having witnessed attacks of it in the stinking grey trenches, brought on not by whiskey but by fear. He had not succumbed himself; Persses did not succumb. At least, not Persses who married wisely and were rewarded with long life and sudden death.

And where was Louisa, the last of the line?

But he had forgotten: she was safe in Wicklow, with his sisters. Not that her mother would consider it safe. A defection, a betrayal. Although she had not used the words, it was what her body had huffed and puffed since she had heard the news.

He was horrified by the realization that love dammed up could eventually fester into hate. Louisa, he had noticed, could no longer bear to call Martina mother and Martina, who yesterday had cried, 'I love her,' this morning had said, 'Do what you like, Robert, it's no concern of mine. Louisa is a teenager, she is not interested in you and me any more. She has discarded us.' At

63

this moment he felt that it was all too late, that love between mother and daughter had already turned to hate. Love was not something that could grow like a weed; it had to be nurtured, cultivated. These two, by wantonly and extravagantly trampling on its tender shoots, had invited its destruction. Now down in Wicklow his daughter was hungry, while by his side the body of his wife had already begun to wither.

Shivering at this horrid image, Robert stretched out a hand towards her. But his fingers recoiled as if the pores of her skin exuded spite. He jumped out of bed to seek oblivion in a sugared pill.

He was shaking uncontrollably when he reached the bathroom.

In the morning, vigorously brushing his teeth, he was thankful to realize that last night's horrors had been no more than that – night horrors. From the kitchen music drifted upwards, and with it the smell of coffee. Breakfast, and a walk through the squares to the gallery – that should blow away any remaining cobwebs. He would miss these morning walks when they moved to the suburbs. About the only advantage of living in this house was the fact that it allowed you to walk most places. If they bought a flat – but Martina wanted a garden.

And you shall have your garden, my love, and you will smile at me again, once we are out of this mausoleum.

She was wearing blue, which he took as a good omen. It was his favourite colour on her, accentuating her eyes, seeming to deepen the pale sheen of her hair. As she offered him coffee, he could detect no strain in her smile.

'I'm winding up the gallery today.'

'Would you like me to come in with you?'

'Yes, please.' She would help to beat down the ghosts that might rise with the dust. 'And we can have lunch somewhere afterwards.'

'I'm sorry I didn't go down with you yesterday.' She touched his hand briefly. 'It was silly of me, but I was annoyed with Lou — '

'Absolutely right.'

'But I'll phone today and beg forgiveness. I can imagine the earful you got yesterday.'

When the telephone rang there was nothing sinister about it. Yesterday, because of the circumstances, Robert might have been forewarned. This morning he went to answer it with his guard down.

'Sorry to interrupt you, sir, at this time of the morning, but I thought I'd get you before you went to work. It's Tom Egan here, sir.'

It took Robert about ten seconds to remember the name and then, painfully, the insides of his throat contracted and he was gasping for air.

He didn't have to listen to what the man said – there was only one reason why he would be ringing him at that hour.

He sat down, then walked twice round the room before returning to the kitchen.

'Not Lou, by any chance?' Martina raised her face expectantly.

'No.'

Beyond her, above her head, unseasonal sunshine streamed in so that her profile shone, was almost transparent.

'It was just some man who wants to discuss a picture with me . . . just some advice.'

The ugliness of what he would have to disclose prevented him from telling Martina the truth. She looked like a picture herself, a figure from one of those Dutch interiors, a lovely woman sitting in her kitchen with sunshine pouring in.

Order, domestic virtues, civilized values: Martina seemed at the heart of these this morning. He must protect her from the darkness of what lay beyond.

'It will mean postponing things at the gallery. I'll tell you what – we'll wait till tomorrow and I'll book a table somewhere smart for lunch. We'll give ourselves a treat.'

Martina listened to Robert's retreating footsteps and stared dully at the kitchen table. Its pine surface, the pale wood brassy in the morning sunshine, was smeared with fingerprints and slides of butter; there were crumbs here and there and a few drops of coffee from the spout of the percolator. She sat inertly, too sad to move. She had no job and no house, having wilfully chucked them both away. She had no child; she did have a husband. She shivered, as if it were cold, but today with the sunshine the basement was unusually warm.

She rose at last and began to tidy the kitchen. She seemed to have spent her life on such domestic chores, but without resentment. She had always rather enjoyed housework, finding something tranquil about restoring order.

Soon she will have no kitchen to tidy. In their new maisonette there is only a largish walk-in cupboard. This, the auctioneer has assured her, is what is called a galley kitchen, very smart and up to date. Martina knows perfectly well that it is nothing more than a cupboard.

Robert doesn't yet know that she has made up her mind and that this maisonette is to be their new home. When they saw it last Saturday, he had demurred. 'It's a bit on the small side, isn't it? You do go from one extreme to the other, Martina – where will Lou sleep?'

'The box room will be quite big enough once I've fitted it out. Modern furniture is designed for small spaces.'

What Robert doesn't know, either, is that the box room will never see the light of day as Lou's room. It will be furnished as a work-room, with a desk and some shelves and clean, unambiguous lighting. There will be a camp bed which Louisa can use but she will not be encouraged to sleep in Martina's new home. Louisa has burned her boats.

Martina rushes from the kitchen and runs without pause up two flights of stairs. She closes the drawing-room door behind her and stands with her back to it surveying the room. She is calmed by the sight of the cool grey walls, the tall windows looking down on her beloved garden. In an extravagant gesture, she presses herself against one of the walls, arms outstretched. It feels dry and smooth and intensely cold. Cold comfort? Rather the reverse.

Over the years this house has offered shelter, pleasure, security and a sense of identity. This house has told her who she is. And now it is to be sold.

Martina sits momentarily, then gets up and begins to move restlessly around. The auctioneer, the same one who introduced her to the delights of the galley kitchen, has told her that a client is coming this week to see it and will probably make a firm offer. Martina felt her heart flop against her ribs. No going back now; too late, too late for that. Surely it is she and not Louisa who has burnt her boats?

The old house, usually so dark and shadowy, is today flooded with sunlight. Whatever angle the winter sun is at, whatever height it has reached in the sky, it has managed to penetrate to the very heart of the house, filling all the rooms and passages with a brittle light. It makes the house seem less narrow, somehow, its character less introverted. Small, square window panes sparkle, ancient wood breathes softly; an air of what is almost frivolity invades the house.

Too late, too late. Martina shakes her head as she thumps her way downstairs; too late for all that. Too late to put your best side forward, your charm on display. You are being abandoned.

For the life of her, she cannot remember what made her take such a decision.

7

Robert didn't want the tea but he was drinking it out of politeness. He often found himself doing unpleasant things through timidity or good manners – he was never quite sure which. Either way, it was not a Persse character trait.

'So you see, sir, I couldn't take the responsibility any longer. It's a shocking disgrace, I don't have to tell you. And we've never had anything like it before at Mount Allen.' The little man looked accusingly at Robert. Perhaps he was going to suggest that Charlotte be dug up and reinterred in less select surroundings. 'If we're lucky, in a manner of speaking, we'll catch the bugger tonight. If not . . .' He took another slurp from his mug.

Robert was acutely aware of the ridiculousness of the situation – two grown men crouching inside a hut in a graveyard in the middle of the night, drinking horrible tea and waiting for the villain to make an appearance. The escapade had a nineteenth-century feel about it – shades of Burke and Hare. And if the fellow did turn up, what would they do? Confront him? If he were mad enough to make a habit of shitting on someone's grave, he was mad enough to take a hatchet to anyone who might want to interfere with his pleasures.

Only by concentrating on the villain could Robert keep the nausea from rising in his throat. That he was a madman was beyond doubt – then surely they should have come prepared? They should have stopped off and picked up a straitjacket somewhere, if there were no machetes to hand. Although, come to think of it, straitjackets were probably redundant nowadays; a large hypodermic depressed into the fleshy part of the buttock was all that was required, the same treatment as for rogue elephants.

Oh, the advances and humanity of modern science. No more padded cells, no more virgin-white straitjackets to be drooled and dribbled down by the mad. Nowadays the mad were pumped full of chemicals which relaxed the muscles and turned the brain cells to cotton wool. Madhouses were pleasant places: no high walls, flowers in the reception rooms, inhabited by gently perambulating vegetables. Yes, and better at that than have them running wild around graveyards. Lock them up, stuff them to the gills with dope, protect us on the outside, and our dead.

The caretaker's hand on his arm shook Robert free from his morbid imaginings and he turned, shamefaced, as if the other had been a witness to their luridness.

'I thought you might have fallen asleep, sir.'

Robert gave the lie to this accusation with a shake of his head and a swallow of tea.

'Did you hear that car, sir? It stopped just outside. This is it – I'm sure of it.'

Robert had heard nothing but he wondered now at the quietness of the night. No sounds reached them from the main road, no sounds from the outside world. Small wonder he had been immersed in such unwholesome fancies, sitting in the damp, surrounded by tombstones.

'Listen. Here he comes now.'

To his surprise, Robert found himself trembling. He leaned forward, peering out the window, trying to distinguish shapes in the darkness outside. The plan was to switch on the outside light, just as the blighter walked in front of the hut, and catch him in its beam, red-handed. Robert had suggested that it would be better to wait and catch him red-arsed.

'And who'll clear up the mess, sir, if you don't mind me asking?' Tom Egan had replied. 'It's not necessary to go that far; a good fright is all that's needed and he won't trouble us any more.'

Tiny sounds were now becoming audible to Robert's ear: the

echo of a footfall rising from the ground, the swish of brushed foliage. Then a weak beam of light and a greyish figure glided, floated into view.

'Now I've got you.' The caretaker's roar made Robert jump. Light flooded on to the cement path and both men blinked in an effort to refocus. The figure stopped, then half turned.

'My God,' Tom Egan breathed damply, 'a woman. A bloody female woman.'

As he started to pull on the warped door, the woman, raising her head like a young horse, turned round and began running back towards the gate.

'Could you believe that, sir, if you hadn't seen it with your own eyes?'

But Robert, slipping the man a fiver, was already out the door. 'That's it then, Mr Egan. I don't think there will be any more trouble. That's the end of that.'

The only light burning when Robert finally got home was Martina's bedside lamp. Although he had spent an hour in the pub, he had drunk little, gagging on a glass of whiskey and replacing it with a glass of beer from which he had merely sipped. Now he looked down on his wife lying on her back, her mouth closed, breathing gently through her nose. Beside her lay a book, crimson dahlias spreadeagled across its open back.

I won't disturb her, Robert told himself. I'll let her sleep, I'll spend the night in the spare room. It would be such a pity to disturb her.

He tiptoed out, leaving the lamp burning in case she woke unexpectedly during the night. Then she might be frightened and call out to him. But Robert wouldn't hear. He intended to take a sleeping tablet; he had need of sleep.

'I was home a lot later than I expected.' Robert kept his eyes on the porridge and cream in his bowl. 'What did you do? I hope I didn't spoil your evening.'

'I wasn't doing anything, anyway.'

'You didn't go out?'

'I went to bed early. I — '

'What time?'

Martina laughed. 'Why the interrogation? I was in bed by nine.'

When Robert raised his eyes, he was shocked by the unmarked beauty of his wife's face, its tranquil expression. What age was she now – forty-three, -four? And yet, no wrinkles. The pale, almost transparent skin covered the bones without a pucker or sag. Charlotte's face had been deeply scored, her daughters' looked quite haggard; even Lou had two frown lines between her black eyebrows. Martina's complexion, however, like the porcelain to which it had so often been compared, reflected the world, taking no impressions.

Perhaps he had been mistaken after all, for surely there would be some visible sign, some dulling of that shining surface? It was impossible to believe that the madness of evil which had prompted such a hideous and obscene action could be concealed inside such loveliness. There was another explanation – she had merely been walking through the graveyard at night, wanting to visit Charlotte's grave undetected, self-conscious about her act of piety – which would also explain this morning's lie.

Even as he fed himself this fantasy, Robert recognized its implausibility, and, even as its falseness echoed inside his skull, it was being pushed aside by a vile image – an image of Martina squatting down, her white haunches glinting in the moonlight, the red of her private parts horribly exposed like a female monkey in a zoo cage.

'Are you cold, Robert?'

'No.'

'Shall I get you some more coffee?'

'Just stop fussing.'

She raised a pale eyebrow and poured herself another cup. 'I'm meeting the auctioneer today. Did I tell you that he has found someone who is definitely interested and wants to come and see the house?'

'We mustn't sell.'

Martina pushed the crumbs on her plate into a circle. 'I thought . . .' She raised her eyes to his face. 'I thought that was what you wanted.'

'I've changed my mind.'

'The money — '

'I don't give a damn about the money. This house is not being sold.'

Another, more fearful image had superseded that of Martina squatting on the grave. It was of Martina and himself squeezed together in a tiny house. They would bump against each other as they moved around; they would breathe in each other's stale, exhaled air; they would be always in each other's hearing, seldom out of sight. At least here they could live in decent separation. They needn't even sleep on the same floor, never mind the same room – or bed. He could make excuses, move up or down.

He met his wife's solicitous gaze.

'Are you feeling all right this morning, Robert?'

'Yes. Why?'

'I just wondered. You seem a bit upset.'

Unlike you, dear wife, who can still smile and smile.

I can divorce her. I don't have to share my house or my life with her. I can go to England and fulfil the residential requirements and get my divorce.

And if she contests it, will you tell the court why you want a divorce? You could sell your story to a tabloid newspaper – they'd love it.

I'll desert her then. Walk away.

What about your daughter, Louisa? What will you tell her when you walk away?

I'll make her life so unpleasant that she won't be able to live here, that she'll be the one to leave.

'Robert, I think you should go back to bed – you're shivering. I'm sure you've caught a chill. Come on, I'll help you.'

'Don't touch me.'

He stumbled from the kitchen, down the passage to his study. He needed a drink, now, this second.

Uncorking the bottle he raised it to his lips, dispensing with a glass.

Let her listen outside. Let her come in and catch him in the act.

Good God – that he should be feeling guilty about having a whiskey in the morning when he thought what she –

But he mustn't think.

He must preserve normality, give himself time to come to some sort of decision, to work out some plan of campaign.

'I'm off now, I'm going into the gallery. There are one or two items . . . Just remember what I said, put off that auctioneer chap, at least for the present.'

He ran up the area steps into the rain. He wouldn't go back for an umbrella. Better get a soaking than risk going back in there where any moment she might open her mouth and begin to tell him things, offer fearful explanations.

He ran along the side of the square. Only when he was around the corner did he pause, gripping his side and drawing air into his bursting lungs.

Recovering his breath, he turned away from the direction of the gallery and began to walk towards the bright shopping streets. Although it was not yet ten o'clock, they were already beginning to fill up.

The rain fell but nobody seemed to mind. It was Christmas week and the world was celebrating. Gold and silver tinsel and multi-coloured lights twinkled at him from every shop window; 'Hark The Herald Angels' followed after him and well-wrapped bodies brushed against him, releasing perfume which mingled with the smell of roasting coffee beans.

At Switzer's he stopped and stared at a notice which read 'This Way to Santa's World'.

They had always brought Lou to visit the Switzer's Santa for he had had a reputation for class, being older, fatter and jollier than the often emaciated and acned species that was employed by the other stores.

Robert moved on, wondering whether it was tears or raindrops which felt cold on his cheeks.

He could not see himself ever going back to that house. He could not imagine himself ever looking on her face again. If he did he might kill her, kill himself, kill both of them.

He walked on through the town, shouldering his way through the crowds, crossing over O'Connell Bridge, where he stopped to stare into the sluggish water with its oily rainbow pools. He wondered how long he could keep going; perhaps he could make it to the countryside and continue on up to the Border where he might eventually pass out and be left to die, with nobody foolhardy enough to approach his body in case it was booby-trapped. He stared into the face of a beggar woman and she, accustomed only to downcast eyes and averted glances, shied away from him.

He turned back the way he had come and wondered what he was going to do. What was to become of any of them?

8

Robert was lunching with his sisters. At first, when Rosamund had rung, he had refused. 'I'm too busy – I've no time for lunching out.'

'Then you'd better make time. It's about your daughter.'

'Lou?' Terror jumped in his throat.

'I can't discuss it over the phone. Meet us in the Shelbourne at one.'

He had forgotten about Lou. Ten days ago he had rung her and told her that they couldn't get together over Christmas as Martina had chicken pox. He had been afraid that she might have come bounding in and he couldn't have that. He couldn't risk her being contaminated.

'We're not celebrating Christmas,' he had told Martina. 'It's too soon after my mother's death.' He thought he mightn't have been able to get the phrase out but he had, and then, before she could make a reply, he had rushed to the study, locking the door behind him. He didn't care now what she thought. Obscurely, he simply felt the need to keep things going, which entailed avoiding her as much as possible. He began to make his own meals, eating things from tins – baked beans, corned beef, digging in with a spoon while he stood at the sink looking out the window. Martina watched him but she said nothing. When he left a room he could feel her eyes on the back of his neck.

Now he stared around him, surprised that civilization had not crumbled, that carefully dressed men still stood behind bars and polished glasses with pristine tea towels. He gulped his whiskey and wondered what news Rosamund had for him. He should have thought; he should at least have rung up. Poor Lou – to have been forgotten so completely.

Bunny and Rosamund were looking forward to a decent lunch. Over the years they had developed into quasi-vegetarians, for among their friends meat eating was considered both barbarous and, latterly, unhealthy. However, the sisters had been reared as robust carnivores and a well-cooked steak could still set the saliva flowing, especially when somebody else was paying for it.

They had insisted on the Shelbourne for it gave them a thrill to eat there, reminding them of girlish fun when they used to get squiffy in the Horseshoe Bar before going on somewhere.

Robert took one look at the menu. 'Let's go Dutch. This place has got very expensive.'

'Don't be such a meany.' Bunny wrinkled her long nose at him. 'We are poor starving artists, after all, and you are a property tycoon. How much are you getting for the house, anyway?'

'I'm not selling.'

'What?'

'We've changed our minds. I've taken it off the market.'

Rosamund stood up. 'Then I think we shall be better off eating in the grill.'

As Robert followed his sisters from the dining-room, he realized that a month ago he would indeed have felt a meany, expecting them to pay for their own lunch. But a month ago his world was still intact, there were still values and decencies to be observed. Since then, his preoccupation had become an obsession, and all of him, his intelligence and will, was focused on hiding from his wife the revulsion he felt for her.

He couldn't bear to have her near him; the thought of her touching him sent a shiver down his spine. Along with this physical distaste, however, there had begun to grow within him a compassion for her. He wanted to understand why she had done it, what had driven her to it. As he lay awake in the spare room where he now slept most uncomfortably on a futon, he puzzled over her and how he could ever broach the subject with her.

He had escaped to the spare room by inventing an allergy to the house mite which lived in mattresses and carpets. Martina, raising an eyebrow as the carpet was removed and a futon purchased, said nothing. Whether she believed in his allergy or not was of no interest to him; he knew that he could no longer lie beside her.

He wondered every night how he could approach the subject. Is there something you would like to tell me, Martina? Did you hate my mother? We all behave peculiarly at times, particularly when we are under stress.

He could clearly imagine her lack of response, a faint shadow of bewilderment crossing her features as he stumbled on and on, forcing him to the bald question: *Why did you shit on my mother's grave?*

It was unthinkable. Despite their vigorous sex life, there had always been a reserve between Martina and him. In fact, it was only in the actual act of sex that her inhibitions seemed to desert her; otherwise, she could be almost prudish, certainly prim. She never undressed in front of him; her underwear was always modestly folded beneath a sweater or blouse; her use of genteel euphemisms had always made Louisa and him laugh. Then how could he – It was unthinkable.

Equally unthinkable, however, was pretending that nothing had happened, keeping his knowledge of what she had done to himself. It had to be confronted, for both their sakes, dragged out into the light of day and examined. There had to be a better explanation than simple viciousness. Or madness. He didn't know which concept frightened him more.

'For goodness sake, Robert, have you gone deaf?' Rosamund's bony finger poked him in the ribs. 'Have you heard a word I've said?'

'Sorry.'

'Considering that it's about your own daughter and that we have closed up and lost a day's trade *and* we end up paying for our own lunch.'

'I'm sorry, Rosamund, and I was only joking – of course I'll pay for the lunch. Now – what's this about Lou?'

The sisters' faces grew even longer. Louisa, they were sorry to have to tell him, had run away. Had left them high and dry, in fact, with no more word of explanation than that pottery was not for her. She had packed her rucksack, kissed them cheerfully, indeed unfeelingly, and walked out the door.

'But where did she go?'

'Back to London, to the bright lights.'

'But she couldn't have any money left.'

Rosamund sniffed. 'Don't you believe that. She has more money than either of us. You are a fool, Robert; you never see anything. Louisa's solvency is the least of your worries.'

Bunny covered his hand with a sandpapery claw. 'Have you any idea who her friends were in London?'

'I don't think she had any; she was working in a hotel, staying there.'

'I wouldn't be so sure. All we know is how anxious she was to meet the postman before we did.'

'And letters did arrive.'

'Poor Martina, this will be too much for her – on top of the chicken pox. That's why we wanted to see you on your own. She knew she was safe with us and, besides, we were teaching her our craft – her future was secure. Bunny and I had actually talked of making her our heir.'

'No, Ros, don't you remember? You've got it wrong. We were going to give her the business as a going concern, Robert, hand over to her when we retired. Now, alas . . .'

'Alas.'

The two women stared at him, the solemnity of their expressions casting their features in an even more equine mould. Rosamund patted his hand. 'Break it gently to Martina. She will need extra solicitude at a time like this.'

'And what about me?'

'You'll be all right, little brother. You're a Persse.'

As he waved goodbye to his sisters, he realized that he was relieved to know that Louisa was once more in London. Once, he had wanted her home in the bosom of her family, believing that she would be safer there. That, however, was before he had eaten of the deadly fruit of the Tree of Knowledge and learned about mothers and daughters and wives.

The air in London would be healthier for her; there she could choose her company: no one would force her to live in close proximity to disease.

And if letters were coming to her in Wicklow, he didn't worry. He knew now that worry had no utility with its implications of power and control. He had put out a hand and watched as cities of straw collapsed in front of him. Like the birds of the air, Louisa's only chance was to spread her wings and throw herself on to whatever current was coming her way.

It was a bitter truth for a father to have to admit to.

He had taken to watching her as she moved around a room. He sat like a cat, his body tense and motionless, only his eyes betraying any animation. If she glanced at him, he dropped his eyes, pretending occupation; he liked to sit at a distance from her, on the other side of the room.

'Shall we go away somewhere for a weekend?' Her voice was gentle. 'It would be nice to get away, to a hotel, or even to the sun.'

'I don't think so.'

'Why not, Robert? This is really the first time we could.'

'What about Louisa?'

'Oh, Louisa.'

When he had told her about Louisa's flight, she had shrugged her shoulders. 'I knew that arrangement wouldn't last.'

She had pretended indifference but he could tell that she was pleased. He had watched the contours of her body soften, heard the meekness in the fall of her step. She didn't any longer snap around the house with great energy and purpose. She was glad that their child was once more out on the waves of the world.

A monster. He was married to a monster. He closed his eyes to blot out her figure, to try to convince himself of the truth of his discovery. All that pale and shimmering beauty undermined

79

it, making him appear the monster to have incubated such thoughts.

'Robert.'

He opened his eyes.

'Robert.'

Before he could escape, she was upon him, leaning over him, her arms coming round him, her breasts softly flopping against him. 'What's happening to us?'

Then, as he raised his arm to throw her off, his hand brushed her nipple, hard and raised. Desire replaced disgust; he pulled her down, fumbling with her clothes. She helped him, opening the buttons with small cool fingers.

He was surprised by the pinkness of the nipples, the blue-white of the skin. He had forgotten.

He stood up, almost knocking her over. 'Take off your knickers. Open your legs.' He relished the brutishness of the language.

She was clinging to him, licking him like a cat. Bitch. He pushed her against the wall and thrust into her. He wondered whether the strangled cry came from him or her and whether it was an expression of satisfied lust or of pain.

The dead smell of spent semen hung on the air. Robert was aware of the foolishness of his stance, trousers around his ankles, shirt sticking out around his buttocks. He searched for a handkerchief and began to dab at his thighs. There had been no difficulty entering her: she had been damp and spongy as a bog. Bitch.

Bending to pull up his trousers, he caught sight of his stricken face in the firescreen. He sat down on the ground. What was happening to him? He had been brought up in a family of women whom he had respected and loved. He had married and had a daughter who had brought him great joy. Even as a schoolboy he had been disgusted by dirty talk. Yet today he had behaved like a savage and had enjoyed it.

I am sick, he thought. I have been poisoned by Martina's malaise. She should be isolated, confined with a bell around her neck before she infects others.

As for me, I am lost, I am beyond redemption.

He reached for the tantalus behind him, then remembered that it was locked. An action taken in another lifetime when it had mattered how much whiskey he had consumed. He got the key from behind *Pilgrim's Progress*, a book that was seldom taken down. The whiskey calmed him as its familiar warmth hit his stomach. Dipping his finger in the glass, he flicked the liquid round the room, trying to get rid of that other smell. He smoothed his hair and looked at himself in the firescreen again. Restored. Sadist restored.

No point in beating about the bush – that's what he was. The sense of power, the awful creeping pleasure, distinct from yet related to the sexual thrill. He had rationed himself today, foregone the pleasure of slapping her head till it shook on its frail neck; of bruising the white, impervious skin. He could imagine the terror growing in her eyes as he yanked back her hair, forcing her to look up into his face.

He found himself trembling suddenly, the glass clinking against his teeth. How terrifyingly fragile a thing was human sanity; there was no great divide between the mad and the unmad. We were all driven mad by the pain of life; some of us were just better at stopping up the dyke. But his finger had come loose; the madness seeping through would soon be increased to a torrent.

If he could find someone to love, but who was there? Charlotte was dead, Louisa fled.

Martina and he had been going to grow old together. Side by side in a little house, their kindness and gentleness to one another would have increased with each passing year, each passing season, each leaf that fell.

He refilled his glass. The pleasure in drinking could begin once the gulping stage had passed. Outside, behind the area railings, there were many brown cardboard boxes, each one filled with empty whiskey bottles. He used to worry about empty bottles once upon a time, a month or a hundred years ago. He used to take one or two out in his briefcase on his way to work in the mornings and throw them in the rubbish bin on the corner. '*Bruscar*', it said on the bin in archaic lettering in that absurd bloody language they were all supposed to speak. Lou would have no need of her Irish now. She would settle down, in Fulham, perhaps, settle down and marry a Brit or a Paki –

Why was he thinking like this? Misanthropy. Woman delights not me, no, nor man either.

And my sodden self least of all.

He had to get a divorce – too late to worry now about what came out. One could be got quickly, he believed, in Honolulu or the Cayman Islands or some such place. He would stand up in front of the black judge and say, 'Your honour, I wish to have my marriage dissolved because my wife desecrated my mother's grave. My wife shat on my mother's grave.'

And beautiful Martina, seeming more beautiful than ever in this land of dusky skins, beautiful Martina would reply with a gentle smile, 'No, no, your honour, my husband is mad, he suffers from delusions. Like all men, he was in love with his mother, and so he cannot accept her death. Grief has turned his mind.'

And he would be carted off to the funny farm for the rest of his natural.

So he was stuck. No divorce, no showdown, stuck. Until he died of alcoholic poisoning or Martina of – In her case it would inevitably be old age. Around the 102-mark. There was an awful indestructible quality about Martina: she would go on and on. He could imagine her like the Venus de Milo, losing an arm here, a lump of shoulder there, but still surviving, smiling imperturbably.

The only thing to do with her was to take her out and shoot her. Well, possibly not, not nowadays. His grandfather could have got away with it but he would have to be more circumspect. A little something in the after-dinner coffee, then drag her out through the dining-room windows and bury her in the herbaceous border. No nosy parker neighbours to report strange goings-on to the police, just the blank indifferent faces of office blocks. And if the police, suspicious by nature and training, were to start asking questions and, wandering round the house in search of evidence happen upon the newly-dug soil, he had a perfect alibi. The Michaelmas daisies had just been taken up to be redivided, or the irises.

He knew damn all about gardening but he had an expert on the premises. 'What needs digging up now, Martina? Are you clearing any flower beds in preparation for bedding plants?'

He thought of the refinement in cruelty which the Nazis had attained, getting their victims in the camps to dig their own graves. Just the ticket for Martina . . . a one-way ticket.

Useful to the last. He must find out too which plants needed a lot of bone meal. No more mean little bags from garden shops from now on; and a better quality of bone meal, to boot.

He cackled, then choked on an intake of whiskey. He was going mad. In fact, could he any longer be considered sane?

It was this drinking.

He stood up and carefully poured what was left in his glass back into the decanter. He lifted the decanter and placed it in its silver prison but, just as he was on the point of turning the key, he noticed how little whiskey there was left, hardly worth making such a fuss about. He stretched out his hand, then withdrew it. No. He walked to the door, paused. What the hell – the decanter needed to be washed, in any case. Swiftly he retraced his steps, took the decanter by the neck and dispatched the liquid. He wiped the dribble from his chin, pleased with himself and his new resolve.

He would not open another bottle until Friday evening. That would be all right; a man, after all, was entitled to a drink at the end of a hard week. Once he had himself firmly in hand.

9

The world had been washed in grey: the sky, the calm waters of the Liffey, the wall of Guinness's brewery and, opposite, the high wall of St Patrick's Hospital.

Dubliners were proud of St Patrick's, its antiquity and its illustrious founder, Jonathan Swift. Aloud, Martina recited the Dean's own words:

> He gave the little wealth he had
> To build a house for fools and mad,
> And proved with one satiric touch
> No nation needed it so much.

Would Robert have been classified as a fool or a madman if he had been admitted to St Patrick's in the time of Swift? Or would they have taken in alcoholics at all in those days?

Martina straightened her shoulders but kept her eyes on the ground as she walked up the hill towards the hospital gates. There was a misty rain falling, silent, hardly seeming to wet and yet soaking through in seconds.

She had been summoned. Dr Morgan's secretary had rung to make an appointment for her.

'What for?'

'Oh, just a chat. Then Robert can join you both for a cup of tea.'

Robert, not Mr Persse. It was supposed to reassure one, all that chumminess.

The trees in the hospital grounds were ancient and dark, the earth underneath dry and rustling. The hospital itself had a dignified central block and a sprouting of incongruous wings around this. There was a lot of glass in these new wings draped in bright, nursery-coloured curtains.

Martina had been surprised at how docilely Robert had agreed to enter St Patrick's. She had been prepared for a battle and had been quite ready to have him committed if that proved necessary. After the incident in the study she realized that as a result of her abstraction she had failed to see that her husband's behaviour could no longer be described as merely strange.

Busy and preoccupied, she had noticed at the periphery of her consciousness that he had changed. There was a furtiveness about him which was new, an inability to meet her eyes. His own were red from the whiskey which he had begun to drink quite openly after breakfast. When he had announced that they wouldn't celebrate Christmas she had been surprised to find that it was that time of year again but indifferent to what would be done to mark it.

Occasionally, through the fog of her introspection, she felt a stab of pity for him as she noticed the suffering which dragged at his handsome features. It was a moment such as this which had moved her to put her arms round him in the study. When he had then demanded sex she had been surprised but undismayed, for it had been a long time and he was still her husband.

It was only afterwards in the bathroom, as she tended her bruised and smarting flesh, that she became aware that his actions had been motivated by aggression, even, perhaps, hatred. 'Get out,' he had said, as she stooped to gather her underwear from the floor.

Martina then made up her mind that if Robert was going to be a nuisance she had better get him out of the way. She was too busy to give him the attention, which in any case could be more skilfully provided by the professionals.

Dr Morgan looked tired, a nerve twitched underneath his left eye. 'The problem is, Martina – you don't mind if I call you Martina? – the problem is that we can't get anywhere with

Robert. He won't co-operate. Nothing wrong with him, he tells us, just likes the taste of whiskey; perfectly happy, no problems. Your proverbial clam.'

'And you thought that I — '

'Might help us, Martina. To get an angle on him, so to speak.'

How could Martina help? Her husband was as much a mystery to her as he was to his psychiatrist.

'You wouldn't mind a few questions . . . since he refused to answer. Would you say, Martina, that you had a happy family life?'

'What's happy . . . I suppose so, in so far as any of us . . . Robert was pleased that we were going to sell the house and move to something smaller.'

'His mother died recently.'

'Yes, but she was very old and Robert and she were never very close. He used to get irritated by her – she was something of a trial.'

'You've only one child? A daughter now living in London? Rather young to be living so far from home.'

'Yes, but that was good news – we had a wonderful surprise with Louisa. We had been worried when she'd gone off at first, especially as she told us she was working as a chambermaid. We thought – well, she was a clever girl. But now it turns out that she was deliberately keeping us in the dark; I suppose she wanted to surprise us. She's been accepted as a student in the Camberwell College of Art. She was over there getting her portfolio together and doing interviews.'

'And you were both pleased?'

'Of course – it's a wonderful achievement. And it was especially exciting for Robert. He wanted to be a painter himself at one time.'

Dr Morgan sighed and stared at the ceiling. 'And the intimate side of your marriage?'

'Yes, fine – until recently. But that's obviously a result of all the drinking.'

'But why does he drink?'

'I don't know.'

He drank because he drank. She could offer no explanation – unless that it was genetic. She believed that some schools of thought offered such an explanation for alcoholism. Anyway, it had been necessary to have him admitted. Dr Morgan had seen the state he had been in.

When she was driving home, Martina realized that she had got her chronology wrong. Robert was already in hospital when Louisa had phoned with her good news. The relayed message had been received by him with blank eyes, his yellowish furred tongue visible between the slack lips. 'Thass good,' he had slurred, sounding more drunk on whatever it was they were pumping into him than he had ever done on whiskey.

Since then, even though they had obviously reduced his drugs, he showed little interest in his only child. He showed little interest in anything, sitting tearing things with his hands: tissues, table mats, newspapers. The deadness of his eyes made Martina look away.

Yet she felt no sorrow for his plight; she visited him from a sense of duty but she was removed from his suffering. Her own great period of mourning and abasement had begun.

On the day of Charlotte's funeral, Martina's body had been shaken by a towering rage. It had been like a fever, starting with a few trembles in the morning and building up to an inferno of passion by the time the funeral service had begun. Mourners started calling to the house in the morning, many of them dressed theatrically in black. They stood around in attitudes of grief, adjuring Robert to be brave. They pressed his hand and shook their heads, fighting back tears. Martina found it incredible that such a fuss was being made over the death of a not very pleasant old woman.

In the church, it had been difficult to breathe with the overpowering scent of cut flowers. There had been organ music, hymns, pleas to the congregation to accept the will of God and to remember with gratitude how long Charlotte had been spared to live among them.

The funeral procession had been stately, the sun coming out for it but shining in a restrained and dignified manner. Even birds had contributed a sweet and final anthem. Sobs had mingled with birdsong as the coffin had been lowered into the earth. 'Steady,' Robert had said and had rushed to put an arm each round Rosamund and Bunny.

On the journey home in the undertaker's large car Louisa had declared that, as the only grandchild, the only representative of the next generation, her sorrow was unique.

That night, when Robert had finally come up to bed, he had found Martina weeping. He had changed the damp pillowcase and then, pushing back her hair, had held her while expressing gentle pleasure that she should feel so upset by Charlotte's death. 'We can share it, darling; that way we can comfort one another.'

And she had thought: Stupid man, stupid and crass. You deserve your fate; you deserve to be a Persse.

For the tears which had fallen on Martina's pillowcase had been shed for another death, another funeral which had taken place some twelve years previously. On that day, the church had been cold and empty except for the handful of mourners huddled near the front. There had been no flowers and no music, and on the altar the priest had paused, fumbling for a name, trying to recall who it was he was burying.

Four people had stood at the open grave – Martina, two aunts and a neighbour.

'Why didn't you put it in the paper, Martina?' Aunt Margaret had asked. 'There would have been a decent turn out if you had put it in the paper.'

'That was Mother's wish.' Martina brazened out her aunt's sceptical stare.

She hadn't put the death notice in the newspapers because she hadn't wanted the Persses to come nosing around. Although Charlotte had been away on holiday, she could imagine her sisters-in-law arriving to pay their respects. Then staying to snicker, noting Aunt Margaret's shabby clothes, the ill-fitting Sunday suits of the male mourners.

And as the little funeral party had stood at the grave, Martina had gripped her hands tightly together and told herself that it didn't matter. Bridie didn't mind, Bridie wasn't feeling anything; she was, after all, dead.

Martina had shaken hands with the priest, then turned to the other three. 'Let me offer you some lunch; I'm sure you could all do with something to eat.'

They had had an uncomfortable meal in a city hotel where the aunts found the food unrecognizable and the wine sour. Then Martina had kissed them goodbye and walked away, closing a door on the past. Or so she thought.

Resolutely she set her mind on the present. All mementoes of the past she destroyed or gave away. She allowed herself no idle moments and, if her mind did occasionally stray, then she blew her nose hard and rang up Freda for extra work.

Not remembering became a habit, effortless after a while. Within a year of Bridie's death, her daughter was able to come upon an old woman in a street or supermarket without her stomach churning with dismay. Then at Charlotte's funeral, closing her eyes as a sunbeam caught her, without any warning a picture of her mother appeared on a screen inside her head. The skin of her face was still pretty; her eyes smiled at her daughter as they had so often done in life.

The face had vanished, and since then Martina had spent hours trying to call it up again. In the large empty house she sat looking out the window, trying to remember what for so long she had forced herself to forget. She followed the sun round the house, moving from room to room and from floor to floor. When the heat switched itself off, she shuffled into an overcoat, for she couldn't be bothered to light a fire any more than she could to cook a meal. Sometimes she forgot the time and had to rush to the car and speed to the hospital to get in before the end of the visiting period.

The house grew dull. Although she did certain tasks without thinking – washing cups, making her bed, she neglected all other housework. Dust lay everywhere; polished floors lost their sheen.

Windows grew smeared as Martina cleared little circles, polishing with the side of her hand so that she might look down on the garden or the square.

She was assailed by waves of sorrow as the past came floating back. Each new image made her cry aloud and shake her head in disbelief at her own behaviour. Why had she denied her mother a decent funeral, a good send-off?

At first in these visions she could see only herself, Bridie had been merely an outline. Then she had hoped that her behaviour might be justified, that the mother whose memory she was trying to retrieve might have merited what she got. The woman who gradually emerged into Martina's consciousness was no monster, however. Bit by bit her daughter put her together, sticking on a smile here, an incident there, fitting in phrases and beliefs.

Her mother had been an ordinary woman, average, one could say. Not very bright, not very beautiful, rearing her daughter on her dead husband's pension without any real hardship for either of them. Average in every respect except in her love for her daughter.

She loved me.

The phrase filled the house as Martina began to say it aloud, at first in wonder and then in ever increasing pain.

In spite of everything, she loved me.

Martina moved around the house, chewing an apple or an unbuttered crust, trying to make sense of the past. The period she recalled most vividly was her adolescence, that epoch of warfare with her mother. Martina had been unhappy then, shy and introverted, seeing her fatherless state as somehow shameful, blaming her father's death on Bridie whom she also blamed for her spots and her indifferent marks at school. Her mother, she now saw, had handled the situation badly, responding to each provocation, raising her voice in disharmony with her daughter's so that they seemed to spend most of the time shouting at one another. Her mother objected to her appearance, her manners, the state of her bedroom. Martina had seethed and vowed revenge.

Now she shivered in superstitious awe at the fulfilment of that vow.

When adolescence had passed, when Martina had left school and got a job in an office, her mother was still around; by now, however, the daughter had stopped noticing. Now she was full of the excitement of her own life: money to spend, boyfriends, clothes, the surging and heady belief that she could do anything. Mother quietly and steadfastly continued to perform her little services – little acts of love: a bottle in Martina's bed at night, clothes collected from the cleaners, a generous ear and a kind, indeed partial, eye. The mother's shining face reflected the daughter's perfection, giving her back an image of herself where nothing was wanting.

And all this was perfectly natural, part of nature's great design. All things had their season and, as the egotism of youth grew ragged, as daughters grew older, got married and gave birth themselves, they turned to their mothers with recognition, and love flowed without complications as it had in childhood.

At forty-three years of age, looking back over her life, this was what Martina believed. Her own life had been moving in that direction when she met Robert. Now, as further scraps of her past came drifting upwards, Martina remembered afternoons in her mother's house with Robert taking tea and the three of them chatting desultorily in the sunshine. And evenings, gathered round the kitchen range, at ease, rubbing along together unselfconsciously.

Things would have been different, my life would have turned out different if – if Charlotte had not happened along.

See that young, pretty, rather silly girl tripping along to be introduced to her future mother-in-law. She is not nervous – why should she be? She is protected under the talisman of love, invincible within its shining circle. Without hesitation she advances upon the large and regal woman, offering her a small pink hand. To her large and ugly daughters, standing shoulder to shoulder, she offers smiles, although sugar lumps would be more appropriate, she feels, so strongly do they resemble highly-bred horses.

It is the last time that she is to feel such frivolity in the presence of her future in-laws; by the end of the evening she is puzzled, even upset.

It is not that anyone has been rude to her – in fact, an impartial observer would probably say that they have been charming. Robert, who is not impartial, certainly thinks so. Martina, however, has the disconcerting feeling that none of them has actually seen her. Her arrival is greeted with insouciance, as if Robert made a habit of arriving home with future wives. Their smiles are polite but indifferent, although their conversation among themselves is quite animated. When Martina makes a contribution, they look at her blankly before fixing their smiles as they begin to listen to her, their courteous caste of features belied by their glazed eyes. Occasionally, Charlotte asks her opinion but she falters in her reply, for their attention has already returned to themselves. They are incurious about her, asking her nothing about herself or her background. When she is leaving, having spoken perhaps three half-sentences, Charlotte, extending a hand, says, 'Do come again, Edwina. It's been such fun.'

When Martina returns home that evening, after she has kissed goodnight – Robert with passion and her mother with affection – she sits in front of her dressing table mirror and laughs at her experiences of the afternoon. She brushes her shining golden hair and is reassured: she must have caught them on a bad day.

Bad days, however, become the pattern. They are simply not interested in her, these Persses, *mère et filles*, they are as indifferent to her presence as to her existence. Yet how can she bring up the subject with Robert who sees nothing? 'Your mother and sisters are not paying me enough attention.' Or, 'I don't think they realize who I am.'

She holds her peace but grows agitated. This is reinforced by her constant exposure, for Robert is a loving if somewhat absent-minded son and brother.

Now she tries very hard. She is not used to being ignored and she is determined to do something about it. She goes to the hairdresser's before a visit; she agonizes over her choice of clothes. She irritates Robert with her endless questions about his family. These bore him, and, anyway, he cannot reply to them for he has never paid much attention to the female natter at home. When he discloses casually that Bunny and Rosamund are about to embark on a new enterprise breeding red setters, Martina runs to the library to get a book on pedigree dogs.

It is all to no avail; she is still invisible to all but one set of Persse eyes. She is not even important enough to them to engender dislike or resentment. It is only years later, when Martina has established her own business and is making more money than Robert, that Charlotte shows hostility towards her, although even then she is more puzzled than anything else by her daughter-in-law's success.

Martina could understand it if Charlotte saw herself as a rival; this is something she might even expect. But to be dismissed without a second glance! She is, after all, far prettier than the girls; she is also younger, more intelligent, better read. She is certainly better company. Why does she not merit even a blink of recognition?

It is some time before she realizes that her failure in their eyes is as simple as it is irredeemable – she is not a Persse.

At first, Martina is amused by this ludicrous egotism. Who are these Persses, anyway? They are not royalty, after all; they have no famous ancestors. They are not even particularly rich, although once, apparently, they were. Why should they feel such an innate superiority? She laughs at their pretensions; she jokes about it with Robert, who admits that yes, they are subject to delusions of grandeur. She tries to shrug it off, to be as indifferent to them as they are to her, but eventually the sheer density of their certainty begins to undermine her. As she sits forgotten in the corner of Charlotte's drawing-room and watches them making such a fuss of themselves, considering with unwavering attention every tiny detail of their uneventful lives, she begins to think: Maybe after all, they are important . . . more important than I can ever be. She begins to feel insubstantial, then inadequate, finally, inferior. And this girl, this product of the modern world who has been brought up in a Dublin suburb, the much-loved only child of doting parents, suddenly finds her head invaded by ancestral voices reminding her of forelocks and the touching thereof.

Suddenly she sees the meanness of her own life, the pettiness of her background. She begins to measure her mother against Charlotte and to find her wanting. She begins to examine and analyse what up till now she has taken for granted.

Mother dresses badly, her teeth are discoloured; she has nothing to talk about except the goings on in Brookfield Avenue. Above all, she is meek. She doesn't bark at shop assistants, she accepts rudeness from the hands of tradesmen. It is this meekness which leads her daughter to believe that she is beyond redemption. Martina may one day learn to project herself like a Persse but for her mother it is too late. She will be trampled on; she deserves to be trampled on because she thinks so little of herself. She will not, however, pull her daughter under with her.

Martina becomes obsessed with the idea of keeping her mother and Charlotte apart. Her stomach turns over at the idea of having to introduce them. She fantasizes about running away, eloping with Robert to some distant inaccessible land. When the introduction is finally made, the weekend before the wedding, Charlotte, gracious and smiling, says, 'This is a real pleasure, Bridie – I may call you Bridie? And I know we are going to be such friends and I am so looking forward to it.' Thereafter, she seems to forget that Martina ever had a mother, which, considering that she rarely notices Martina, either, is not surprising.

But Martina does not relax. For the next six years keeping Bridie away from the Persses is a real preoccupation. She comes to realize that her mother is not the innocent she once thought: there is her stubbornness, for example, verging on the selfish. She insists on having her hair tightly permed in the old nineteen-forties style; she refuses to drink anything except sweet sherry and then appallingly raises her glass and says, 'Good health, now, though it's far from sherry I was reared.'

She says it every single time until Martina can barely stop herself from screaming.

Martina is a dutiful daughter and, once a week, from the time Louisa is six weeks old, she brings her to see her grandmother. The visits are invariably marred by bickering, for Martina resents the time spent on them; they always put her in bad form and she comes away with a string of complaints against Bridie, but uneasy, somehow, at her own behaviour.

Occasionally, when she knows none of the Persses is around, she asks her mother home. Bridie, it must be said, does not seem to enjoy these visits as she sits on the edge of her chair, coughing dryly into a closed hand and patting her hair.

If Martina sometimes stops to examine her behaviour, if a realization of its baseness creeps into her consciousness as a blush of shame creeps up her neck, she shakes herself and reassures herself with the fact of her mother's utter hopelessness. Besides, there is time: things will change; there are years ahead to put things right.

But there are not. Louisa is only five when Bridie suddenly dies. At first, Martina does not believe it. She calls the neighbour who brings the news a liar; she runs from the mortuary chapel where they force her to go. Then she thinks that *she* will die. She lies down on her bed, sure that this pain will annihilate her, that nobody can survive it. It is only when Louisa's sobs have turned to hysteria, when the child's tears splash on to her face, that she knows that she cannot die yet. She gets up, goes to the bathroom where she vomits into the lavatory bowl; she wipes her mouth, takes her little daughter in her arms and begins to soothe her.

Thereafter, she does not mourn – why should she? Mothers don't die, at least not until their daughters give them permission to do so. Bridie has been too casual, slipping off like that and at barely sixty-five. From this moment, Martina shuts out the past and throws away the key. What she doesn't realize is that like a boomerang it returns, to lodge, a lump of iron in her heart.

When the sunbeam struck Martina in the church on the day of Charlotte's funeral and Bridie's face shone in the golden light behind her closed eyelids, she was overcome by such a desolation that she could sense it physically dragging her down into the flagged ground. As she slumped, she found Rosamund's steely fingers clutching her arm. 'Pull yourself together.' There was disapproval in the whisper. For once, Martina was indifferent to a Persse opinion; she was recalling with disbelief, then with mounting horror, the details of Bridie's burial service.

It was the beginning of her journey into the past. Charlotte's exit, like her life, engendered fuss and hullaballoo. The widespread and voluble displays of grief, the letters and floral tributes and lovingly remembered anecdotes, made it appear as if her death had indeed created a vacuum it would be impossible to fill. And with each new expression of loss which Martina endured, she was reminded of her own final act of betrayal – her refusal to put Bridie's death notice in the newspapers. This seemed worse than anything which had gone before, so pointlessly cruel, such an inhuman act of omission.

Martina was stunned by her sorrow. Robert, misinterpreting its source, found nothing odd in her behaviour which, in any case, was more or less unchanged. She cooked meals and sewed curtains and tended her garden, hardly recognizing her sorrow which manifested itself as a physical pain – she ached from head to foot. This soon eased, the quality of her sorrow changing as she rediscovered her love for her dead mother. Up till now she had believed that this emotion was something that had predeceased Bridie by about a decade. She began to touch her loss . . . *If only*, she would say to herself, *if only*. And eventually all the if onlys appeared to join together and lead her to the giant-sized figure of Charlotte, sitting Buddha-like, arms folded, smiling malevolently.

Now hatred overwhelmed her sorrow. She would find herself shaking with rage as she thought of her mother-in-law's behaviour over the years. She ground her teeth as she lay under Charlotte's son, listening to his silly endearments, digging her fingernails into his shoulders, wishing him to suffer for his blindness.

When Louisa had left home, she had thought: Good girl, you've escaped – not analysing what she imagined her to be escaping from.

On the third day after Charlotte's burial she was in the drawing-room, looking across at her husband and daughter who sat together, dark heads bent over an old photo album. She listened to their conversation.

'I never knew Granny played tennis.'

'She was a wonderful athlete. She could ride and skate and she was a great shot. Look – she looks rather like you in this one. The way she holds her head.'

'Is that you, Dad? Golly – look at that hat!'

Martina laid down her sewing and soundlessly left the room. She began to walk around her beloved house but tonight it offered no consolation. 'Persse,' shouted the walls; 'Persse,' sniggered the windows.

Without realizing what she was doing, she grabbed her car keys and headed down the garden towards the mews. She was behind the wheel and the little red car headed away from town, apparently of its own volition. When it stopped in front of the gates of Mount Allen, she wasn't particularly surprised.

With automatic steps she crossed the stile on to the path under the yews.

She was looking down at Charlotte's grave, the rough edges of the newly-dug earth catching the dying light of day. Her body grew hot, fiery; her chest heaved as she struggled for breath. She cried out like some night creature and flung herself forward.

Then she was walking away, limp, but with such a sweet sense of relief surging through her.

Martina, with much practice in thought control, had no difficulty now in not acknowledging her deed. And so delightful was the lightness that pulsed within her that it was easy to deny thought in sensation. So this was why Robert drank, why others shot heroin! Her delight was momentarily sobered by a shaft of moral righteousness as she thought how irresponsible was the behaviour of so much of the human race.

She noticed herself improve, grow less nervous. She stopped seeing Charlotte and she put Bridie away for the time being.

97

That was unfinished business and Bridie would be retrieved at some later date, but for the moment there was Robert to be consoled.

Now that she saw him, she was moved by his vulnerability, by a sudden hunted look which said 'Help me'. Martina did not turn away; she determined to put their lives to rights.

With this in view, she went about selling the house, divesting herself of her business. She thought that, if she could get rid of, pare down, throw away, she and Robert might return to the simplicity with which the early days of their marriage had been imbued. Looking back, these now appeared to Martina as happy days.

And for a while it worked, or seemed to, until Louisa's defection and Robert's really heavy drinking began.

When Robert told her that Louisa was safe in Wicklow, as he put it, Martina had experienced despair. That her perfect, impervious girl should run home vanquished would have been hard to take, but that she should turn to the Persses, run to them, her tail between her legs, was more than her mother felt she could bear. She had eyed the gas oven then; had stared long and hard at the exhaust pipe of her car. But her impotence was total – she could not even raise a hand to free herself from her despair.

A journey to Mount Allen did not lessen her depression but it did help her to realize that she had been wrong to think that she could put the present to rights while ignoring the past. Louisa's betrayal she now saw as a mirror image of her own betrayal of Bridie and, begging her mother's forgiveness, she plunged herself once more into the past.

She had deposited Robert in St Patrick's as much for her own convenience as for his safety. Though she visited him in hospital, her thoughts were absent, and, although at this period an outsider might see only a woman mooning around, her life had in fact become highly organized.

She pursued the past with rigour and discipline. She flinched from nothing, facing her own record of neglect, and bravely putting it against Bridie's continuing acts of love.

At night she sometimes wandered in the garden searching the sky, scanning its red polluted glow for some clue that might explain Bridie to her, and herself to Louisa – the whole apparently unstoppable, meaningless merry-go-round.

'Are you out there somewhere, Mother?' she would call, gazing at a star that shone more luminously than all the others. 'If you can hear me, please forgive me . . . it was all an accident.'

But while the accident had obscured love, it had not destroyed it, and this fact Martina now began to hold at her heart where it raised the temperature and caused the beginning of a tentative thaw.

She emerged from the past like an invalid recovering from a long and debilitating illness. Her smile wobbled a little; her pallor was even more marked. She moved around the house with faltering steps, touching surfaces, resting her eyes with gratitude on the many familiar objects.

And there was much to be grateful for. For a month, two months, every night she had begged her mother's forgiveness; now she realized that she must begin to forgive herself. The past could not be undone: like the dead it was beyond her reach. It need not, however, be denied; she was Bridie's daughter as she was Louisa's mother, and within this continuum her sins lost some of their enormity. Bridie's genes had betrayed Bridie. The daughter in loving the mother must logically learn to accept herself.

And there was Louisa's triumph to celebrate, independent in London and launched in her career. Once she had admitted the past, Martina found that she could now fantasize about the future, and not so much fantasy when you looked at Louisa and saw the sureness of her vision. Louisa wanted to paint, with the sort of passion Martina had never felt for anything . . . or anybody. Had she been in love with Robert or was it, at nineteen, that she had been in love with herself? Poor young girl – her image of herself had cracked so easily. A few scornful laughs and it lay shattered and she had been unable to put it together again. But Louisa was made of sterner stuff: Louisa's self-esteem was no mere veneer, it was solid and unshakable.

'And you can be proud of that,' Martina told herself. 'You thrust her into the rough and tumble of life; you stuffed your ears and hardened your heart against her baby cries so that she might learn, if not to bite the hand that fed her, at least to complain about the quality of the food.'

Louisa at least would be all right.

And Robert?

When her thoughts turned to her husband, Martina felt the familiar nervous burping begin in her chest. The truth was, she didn't know what to do about him. Every day she went and sat in the hospital cafeteria, holding his hand while they drank cups of tea. She would tell him things. 'The garden is looking green – I'll soon have to start cutting the grass.' Or, 'There was a new girl on the square last night.'

He would look at her and yawn. His teeth seemed to have got longer, the gums receding scummily. He was beginning to look hollow and old.

He was off medication, the doctors said, but he still appeared dazed. Sometimes he would nod off, or seem to, as she was speaking. His hand under hers would be slack and damp. Her own fingers would recoil but she would force them back down. She told him things to which he did not respond. He had withdrawn himself, and she didn't know if she had sufficient will, love, whatever it was that was needed to bring him back.

10

Robert found now that he spent part of every day thinking about his wife. So thoroughly did he dissect her that when she arrived for her afternoon visit he was recurrently surprised by her pale beauty. Surely there should have been some mark, some bruising? Her inviolability made her seem more alien, more of a puzzle. Did the havoc which the heart wreaked not then show on the face? How could the brow, the mouth, the eyes, remain untouched when such passion seethed underneath? Or perhaps it was just plain madness. Mad Martina striding through the world like Charlotte Corday, her brow unruffled, her hands unclenched.

Robert looked out from his prison and snickered at this irony.

He had begun to see his world as encompassed by the grey hospital walls. These were the boundary of his universe and inside the inhabitants strode, strolled or crawled. It was not unpleasant with no responsibilities, no decisions to be made. The doctors were a nuisance with their persistent, silly questions but the company was OK. The really depressed tended to keep to their rooms while the elated were too high to cause any bother. It was to those recovering that one had to give a wide berth: Robert didn't mind the odd conversation with Napoleon Bonaparte but sober civil servants he had had enough of in the outside world.

In the last week the nurses had stopped throwing pills down his throat. He was glad of this for the pills had made him muzzy-headed, taking the edge off his powers of analysis, and analysis was what interested him now.

His greatest relief had come with the knowledge that he no

longer felt responsible for Martina. When she came to visit him, seating herself across the table, stretching out a hand towards him, he found himself viewing her as a specimen. All that unfocused fear for her which he had lived with through their marriage had dissipated once she had done the unthinkable. All those years of watching and worrying had not prevented it, and so his failure had freed him. He wondered disinterestedly what she would do next or if that one monstrous act had righted her, set her back on an even keel. But his speculation was purely intellectual, his emotions were not engaged.

About himself he did not wonder in the least. His future was out of his hands and the tick-tock of the present provided him with enough diversion.

Robert had never taken the world for granted: he had always been astounded by its diversity, its random bounty. He had viewed mankind with benign interest, marvelling at it in the manner of the Prince of Denmark. He might have thus continued in abstracted placidity except that his eye had been caught and held by Martina's beauty. Then there was little Lou, a rib around his heart, and Robert became embroiled in the pleasures and the pains of the uxorious.

Now, however, all this had changed and Martina had moved into a different perspective. He knew this once he realized that she no longer disgusted him. He viewed her behaviour as he did the human sacrifices of the Incas or the death by exposure of Chinese female infants: it did not upset him nor even surprise him. For him, it had assumed academic interest – he wanted to know why.

Why, he walked around the hospital grounds asking himself, why do people behave so variously? Why does what disgusts me elevate you? Is morality mere fashion, dependent on the era and the hemisphere and the number of mod cons in your empire?

Robert was having a stimulating time. If Dr Morgan thought his smiling face manic, if the nurses shook their heads when he sat alone, refusing to join in the basket weaving, if Martina looked at him with shadowed eyes, it did not diminish his pleasure. He was rejuvenated – invigorated and delighted with life in the loony bin. The pity was it now seemed to him that he had wasted so many years outside. Time did not hang heavy on his hands; there were not enough hours in the day to study, analyse, speculate. Robert had discovered the pleasures of pure cerebration, the strength of its autonomy: within his comfortable barrel he wanted for nothing.

When Louisa came, she found him in his room looking out the window, his back towards her. His forehead rested against the glass, his arms hung limply by his side. She, unaware of the excitement of his intellectual preoccupation, saw only the flecks of dandruff on his once fastidious shoulders.

'Daddy.'

He turned round, staring abstractedly.

'Come on, Dad, stop pretending you don't know who I am.'

But for a moment he hadn't. Painfully he wrenched his mind back to the mundane.

'Hello, Louisa.'

'That's better. Don't I get a kiss?'

He pecked at her forehead, wondering crossly what she was doing here. He seemed to remember that she was now living in London.

'How are you, Dad?'

'Fine.' Already he was beginning to feel agitated. Today was a busy day: there was his morning session with the doctors and then the group therapy when it was impossible to concentrate amidst all the nattering. He really couldn't afford this inter-ruption.

'You don't seem all that glad to see me.'

'The fact is, Louisa, I'm a bit pushed for time.'

'Oh, come on.'

'If you could come back tomorrow.'

'Daddy.'

The wail stopped him. What was there about it? It reminded him of – oh, God.

Desperately he forced his thoughts back – back where they belonged, to an examination of *la condition humaine*. Think of those tribes in Papua New Guinea, which used to be known as New Guinea, just as Kenya was always called Keenya when he was a boy. And when had the inhabitants of the Philippines started speaking American English? Overnight, apparently. He had heard them on television one night, twanging away like the natives of North Dakota. Surely that meant that they could hardly be called Philippines any more? Named after Philip of Spain, who certainly wouldn't have spoken American. When and how had it happened? He certainly –

The arms that came round him were boyish and muscular, strong too, he realized, as he tried to pull away. The womanly bosom he now found himself drawn against contradicted those arms and was in turn contradicted by the smell – oh, that smell! As it enveloped him, he experienced the sensation of being transported backwards through time. It was an asexual smell, a child's smell, clean because children never seemed to smell of corruption as adults so often did. A smell with overtones of grass and forbidden penny bars. Hard, black bars, guaranteed to break one's teeth. Called cough-no-mores.

He closed his eyes tightly. A little girl, a little daughter in a white and blue spotted dress threw out her arms. He lifted her up and buried his head in the cotton dress, nuzzling.

It was so simple.

It was all so long ago . . . a hundred years?

Longer in terms of misunderstandings and recriminations and pain.

'Little Lou,' said Robert, stroking his daughter's hair. 'My little Lou.'

Martina was worried for she believed now that her decision to tell Louisa about her father's illness had been mistaken. Initially, she had protected her daughter. For over a month she had forged Robert's signatures to their joint letters and offered excuses for his absences when Louisa phoned.

As she returned more fully to the present, however, and as her attention focused on Robert, she thought that a visit from Louisa might perhaps help him for she knew by now that she was powerless to do so.

Once she had posted the letter she fretted. What if its contents unsettled Louisa to such an extent that she wanted to come home and thus abandon her career? However sick Robert was, Louisa could not be sacrificed.

When she got the phone call she assumed that Louisa was ringing from London.

'You should have told me straight away – I'm not a child any more.'

'I just didn't want to upset you. And I'd hoped that he'd be out sooner.'

'You put him in.'

'Yes, but – '

'Anyway, we'll talk about it later, I'm going to the hospital now.'

'But – are you in Dublin?'

'You don't imagine I'd hang around over there once I got your letter?'

Martina ran to the linen cupboard to find scented sheets and soft towels. In Louisa's room, she flung the window open wide to banish all traces of mustiness. She found a fluffy rug to comfort bare toes; she scoured the garden for early flowers and made a posy for the bedside table.

In the middle of her preparations, a sudden pain forced her to sit on the bed as a vision of Bridie filled her head. 'Look,' Bridie said, 'I've painted your room while you were away on holidays. Do you like the colour, pet? And I got you a new bedside rug – it's not real sheepskin but the shop said it was just as warm and would wear better. Feel it.'

The mother whom she had so successfully banished for some twelve years was now Martina's constant companion. She accompanied her round the empty house, she looked down at the bruised garden with her; she shared her meals, hunks of cheese

105

and tomatoes, eaten from the fist as they wandered up and down the tall staircases, in and out of dusty, neglected rooms.

'The house looks awful.' Louisa threw a haversack on the drawing-room floor. 'What's going on? It's filthy.'

'I suppose I have been neglecting it . . . your father – it's hard to keep things going.'

Martina was not paying much attention to what was being said; all her attention was focused on the sight of her daughter. She was delighted with what she saw. In some indefinable fashion Louisa had changed: she might still look like an adolescent boy but she was now a woman. Her mother was sure of it.

Her poise was womanly as was her calm and level gaze. Her black, androgynous garments, even her schoolboy boots, did not disguise a new, relaxed assurance. Perhaps over dinner tonight they could talk. Martina would tell her things, explain about the past. Together they could work something out with regard to Robert.

'I must have a kip. I was at Heathrow at eight this morning and I was on standby until one. Are there sheets?'

'But, darling – aren't you hungry?'

'I've eaten. We can talk in the morning. I'm seeing the doctors at eleven but I think we'll have to have a discussion first. Dad's no more an alcoholic than I am, I could see that this afternoon. There are problems there – I don't know. Maybe it would be better if you two split up. Anyway. Call me around seven.'

Martina sat, a foolish smile on her face, as Louisa closed the drawing-room door. She felt foolish, too, and inadequate. No, more than that, she felt vanquished, done up by her own foolishness. Although Louisa had found the house neglected, to Martina's eyes it was full of the ill-judged signs of preparation: a bottle of wine warming on the table, fresh towels and soap in the bathrooms and downstairs in the kitchen a mound of viscous and bloody meat lying in wait for tonight's dinner.

Martina had spent an hour in the morning fighting down nausea, breathing through her mouth so that she did not have to smell the horrid dead smell as she hacked the flesh from the bone, tearing fat from muscle. Now she could tip it into the dustbin and consume instead her usual supper as she wandered round the house.

Perhaps she had been presumptuous in her expectations or perhaps her timing had let her down yet again. As with Bridie, so with Louisa.

She had thought that at last her daughter and she could be friends, now that Louisa had come through, had proved her independence, snapping her fingers at all of them. At last she could let down her guard, for Louisa was too strong today to be damaged by the excesses of maternal love.

Foolish. And dishonest. Was she not looking for her reward for a job well done? Did she not now want to fling thongs around her daughter to secure her to herself? She had spent all these years preparing her for flight; why then should she complain to see her daughter soar with such surety?

Let her go.

There was something else, though. Over the years Martina had grown used to Louisa's contempt, not allowing it to worry her, telling herself that it was all part of the on-going battle between parent and child. Today a young woman had walked into her kitchen and looked at her with the same contempt, and this had not been so easy to dismiss. There had been no hysteria in her daughter's eyes; the contempt had been considered, objective and quite grown up. It could not be ignored.

She must go to Louisa; sit her down and force her to listen while she explained. Explained what?

Martina drew back from the imagined confrontation, fearful of exposing herself to questions and analyses which might put into words what churned around in an unformed glutinous state inside her brain. She had to have more time. Perhaps it would be better to let Louisa go back to London; it would give her mother time to prepare – to think.

Martina left her daughter and turned her attention to erasing from the house the more ostentatious signs of welcome. As she was forcing the cork back into the bottle of wine, however, Louisa's words came back to her. 'Maybe it would be better if you two split up.'

No husband, either?

And would he, too, be whisked off before she could offer him a word of explanation, before she could reach out a hand to wipe away the bitter lines from around his dear mouth?

If Louisa had her way, she might never see either of them again.

Frantically, she began to search for her keys. Finding them, she ran to the back door, then across the shadowed garden. She knew every traffic light between the house and the hospital, every bend in the road, every pothole.

She tore down the lane, then settled at the traffic lights to drive at a more sedate pace: past the convent where nuns kept all night vigil, being summoned by bell to pray for the sins of the world; past the National Maternity Hospital, where cries of pain were choked by tears of joy as new life yelled lustily and slippery little bodies plopped on to waiting breasts; down to the old dark Liffey and on to the quays where a few cheap shops still had their lights on, forlornly looking for late custom.

At Guinness's Brewery she closed her window against the stench of hops; then she was at the hospital gates.

They were locked. She began to pull at them, her fingers making no impression on the decorated iron.

'Let me in,' she shouted, banging her keys against them. 'Let me in – I've got to see my husband.'

'What's all the commotion? What's going on here, at all?' The two policemen seemed to rise from the shadows. They came and stood on either side of her, one of them playing the beam of his torch up and down her body and bringing it to rest on her face.

Martina blinked. 'What?' she asked blankly. 'Sorry, what did you say?' She stared uncomprehendingly at the phalanx of blue chests which seemed suddenly to have cut her off from the outside world.

'You haven't been on the bottle, now?' The younger guard,

noting her appearance which bespoke respectability, even money, felt it safe to offer this sally.

'I seem to have got confused, somehow. My husband is a patient here and I just got mixed up about visiting hours. I didn't realize it was so late.'

They escorted her to her car and stood to wave her off as if she were a child on her first day at school. In her preoccupation, Martina hardly noticed them. She would find it difficult to sleep tonight, difficult to wait until visiting time tomorrow when she could see Robert and tell him that she loved him and how wrong she had been not to tell him so. To tell both of them so, Louisa and Robert, to envelop them in her love, weave it round them, a bulwark against the world. She would make amends, though. Give her a chance and she would make amends.

11

Martina's mood this morning was elegiac. The seasons had changed and winter, her time, had scurried off without its usual lingering farewell. She looked at the crisp, clear day without pleasure; she did not feel up to the robustness of spring.

Yesterday Louisa had gone back to London. During the two days of her visit Martina had avoided her, skulking in her bedroom or pretending occupation when she saw her daughter approach. If only she had had more courage.

Now, however, she was resolved to secure Robert to herself before he, also, fled. She would force him to listen, tell him of her needs, of her love, beg him to come home and give her another chance.

'What are you afraid of, anyway?' Louisa had cornered her for ten minutes at the airport where there had been no escape. 'Why don't you loosen up? If you don't love Dad, then get out – you'll do less damage that way. If you do, for God's sake raise the temperature a little. If he hadn't resorted to whiskey, he'd have died of frostbite.'

Martina acknowledged the truth of that. She would accept all blame for Robert's drinking, admit to him that she had driven him to it but that things would be different from now on, if she were given a second chance.

When she arrived at the hospital she was surprised to find him standing on the steps and not, as usual, inside the steamy café.

'Let's go for a walk, Martina. I want to talk.'

How had she ever doubted the existence of telepathy or of omens, either? Looking up at him, she saw that the film

110

of abstraction had gone from his eyes: he had returned from wherever it was he had been.

They followed a path that led away from the hospital into a wood streaked with sunlight. The stillness of the morning exaggerated their footsteps, making them sound like an army on the march. Martina looked down at the offending feet.

'Will we sit over here?'

Robert swept past the bench, each stride a small explosion of energy.

'I'm leaving this place today; I'm coming home, Martina.'

'Did Dr Morgan – '

'He'll be glad to get rid of me. There's nothing wrong with me, Martina.'

She nodded her head in vigorous agreement.

'Louisa talked sense into me; she made me see things the way they really are. And last night I came to a decision. Martina.' Swinging round, he placed an arm on each of her shoulders, turning her to face him. 'This must be a new beginning.'

'Oh, yes.'

'From now on, we must have everything out in the open. No more deceptions, no more evasions. It's our only hope.'

Evasion, deception . . . hope. The words tore into Martina's chest, causing a choking sensation. She opened her mouth for air.

Robert looked at the lovely stricken face, then quickly looked away. The hand within his fluttered, then lay dormant, hopeless.

'Martina, you must realize, whatever else happens, that I love you.'

She put her arms around him, pressing but hardly making an impression against his bulk. He was conscious of the difference between this and Louisa's embrace. Hers had been tough, somehow, with a confidence that came from nothing more than the condition of youthful flesh.

He could sense within this poor body the germ of decay. Outwardly, it was still a thing of beauty, could still give joy, but Robert was chilled by premonition as he touched, or thought he touched, a slight curve in the once unbent spine.

111

How foolish it was to think of brave new worlds at their age. He must be content with tenderness instead of truth, compassion in place of understanding.

And he had had such hopes.

He could feel the depression, like catarrh, begin to fog up his head. He released himself and offered his hand.

'Take me home, Martina.'

'I will, my darling, I will.'

But where home was, Robert was no longer very sure.

'What a pity the sun's gone in.'

'Yes.'

The sky was low over the square; in the crevices of steps, the wind had formed secret caches of litter. Above the steps, the brightly painted door seemed brazen. This homecoming was familiar, depressingly so to Robert.

In the inner hall he stood, looking up at the staircase and the Venetian window beyond; through it, the grey sky stared back at him, malevolently. Unusual for this house: the air smelt not of flowers but of some chemical sweetener.

'It's good to be home.'

'Come on, Robert – it can't be that bad.' Like a schoolgirl who had escaped punishment, Martina was full of high spirits.

He allowed himself to be led downstairs to where a fire was burning in his study. He looked around him blankly at the walls, his desk, his chair with its blue and white cushion. He looked at his wife as she raised her head from attending the fire to smile at him.

What was he doing here?

The tenderness which he felt towards Martina as she clung to him in the hospital grounds had disappeared and been replaced by a dawning belief that he had been tricked. Resentfully he looked at the smiling face, the aura of brisk confidence emanating from the stance and expression of the body. Invincible, inviolable.

He was all muddled up. Damn Louisa. If she hadn't come

barging in he would still be in his hospital room happily grappling with The Problem of Being.

She had barged in, however. She had shouted and wept over him, demanding that he see her. 'I love you, Daddy – you're the only one I have. And I'm going to get you well – if I have to devote the next ten years to it, I'll make you better.'

'What about college?' The worry stuck through his abstraction.

'Who cares about college? I don't, neither do you. She's the only one who'll worry about that, about the loss of her reflected glory.'

'Don't talk about your mother like that.' The reprimand had been automatic.

'Forget it, Dad, that's all over. I'm grown up now and I'm finished with her. My only interest in her is to see that she does right by you.'

Robert could see, however, that she was not grown up. The lips trembled, the eyes were filled with dismay and bewilderment as she spoke of her mother.

Robert came out of his torpor then, determined to save his daughter. He saw how selfish he had been, how young she was, how much in need of a mother still. Martina was sick but, if she could be cured, Louisa might then find the mother she had never really had.

At that moment it had all seemed simple and straightforward. He would confront Martina, thrash it out with her and persuade her to see someone, a psychiatrist or counsellor of some kind. Then he could explain things to Louisa, telling her not everything, but enough to allow her to understand that her mother's apparent coldness was involuntary, a symptom of her condition, and nothing to do with lack of love. He had had his rest cure; he was resolved to sort out the emotional tangle of all three lives.

What resolve can withstand the curve in the spine of a beautiful woman? Osteoporosis, menopause, hair sprouting along the lovely Grecian line of jaw . . . He watched in horrified fascination as she disintegrated behind the closed lids of his eyes.

And he remembered the girl, not much older than Louisa,

113

who had walked so jauntily beside him, who had said so lightly with a shake of her shining head, 'Your mother really is a weirdo, Robert.' He knew then that Louisa was his daughter, but the debt he owed her mother was the greater . . . And Martina was his first love.

Which left him now no further on than when he had gone into St Patrick's; and with Martina still playing happy families at the hearth.

'I'm afraid Louisa is rather cross with me.'

She was still tending the fire, and with her back towards him he could not see her face, but the familiar falseness in the voice gave him the courage to speak.

'I think it's time we had a talk, Martina – leave that. Louisa needs help, you know, and it can only come from us.'

'No need for such solemnity, I hope.' She had turned to face him, sitting back on her heels, girlish, winning. He knew this Martina of old. 'Lou's just a teenager – like any other. In fact, she's a lot better than she was. Have you noticed she's started to let her hair grow?' Her laugh sounded like ice splintering.

'No, that's not good enough. Louisa is wonderful – I don't know how she came through so well, considering the upbringing she had. No – ' He put out a hand to stop an interruption. 'My fault as much as yours. I acknowledge that.'

'Robert. For goodness sake. There's nothing wrong with her. I know she went through a bad patch and she resented me for a while, but that's natural enough. And we're the best of pals now. We had a super few days last week. Really super.'

Even in his preoccupation Robert paused to wonder where it was Martina picked up her odd vocabulary. From the television, perhaps, or the romances that she so avidly and secretly read. In the past he used to note that their usage would increase with her unhappiness, so that the more miserable he knew her to be, the more she would struggle to appear happy and normal and nice. As if she had a duty to live happily ever after, like the characters she read about.

They couldn't go back to that. It was unthinkable.

'Stop it.'

'Pardon?'

'Stop it, for God's sake. I can't stand it.'

'Robert – what's wrong?'

'This whole sham. Just stop pretending, Martina. Be honest for once. How can we ever sort out this whole mess if you won't be honest?'

She stood up, backing away from him into the wall. Her cheeks were flooded with colour, giving the strange impression of a lovely doll suddenly coming to life.

'Martina.' He stretched out a hand. 'Don't be frightened.'

'I'm not frightened.' That awful humourless laugh again. 'Whatever gave you that idea?'

'You need help, darling.'

'*I* need help? What precisely did you have in mind?'

'Please don't make it so difficult. I'm only suggesting that you see someone . . . a professional person.'

'You mean a psychiatrist. Do you find it difficult to say the word, Robert?' She came back towards him across the room and stood over him. 'Now, of course I understand what's going on. It's a simple question of revenge, isn't it? Because of your alcoholism – and I'm not afraid to say the word – I put you in St Patrick's, and in order to get your own back you are now trying to suggest that it is I who need help, that it is I who am sick. Well, it won't wash. There's nothing wrong with me, I've nothing to hide. You're the one who's got the problems.'

Even through his anger, which had him shaking, ears filled with noise and eyes smarting, he noted the physical transformation in his wife. She stood, arms akimbo, the innate grace of her body revoked by aggression, her eyes opaque as a winter sea, her skin seeming greasy, the very pores enlarged and coarsened.

She was ugly, the words she spoke were ugly, the tones in which she spoke them discordant. Looking at her, Robert had no difficulty in believing that she had committed that ugly deed. And why had he never noticed her stubby fingers, splayed now across her arms like small, pink worms?

'It's no good, Martina – I know.'

'What? What do you know? Not very much, I'd say. There's nothing to know.'

Every word she spoke, every denial she uttered, made his task easier, turning her into an alien being, causing him in the end to express himself with a brutality that he had never intended.

'You can't have forgotten already; it was fairly spectacular, even for you, Martina. You shat on my mother's grave, Martina, that's what you did. You shat on it.'

It was out. He was trembling, his stomach heaving, forcing tears into his eyes. But his mouth was empty. It was out.

Martina spat. The slimy globule landed not on him as it was intended, but on the front of her elegant cashmere frock. He stared at it, mesmerized.

'You're mad – mad.' She was screaming now. 'I'm going to ring Dr Morgan and get him to come and lock you up. He'll put you in a straitjacket and lock you up. You're a madman.'

'You did it, Martina, you did it.'

She fled from the room, blundering against the jamb of the door. He let her go, listening to her footsteps sounding heavy and clumping as they pounded upstairs. His Martina had moved as if wind-propelled.

When he looked down at his hands he noticed that they had stopped trembling.

12

Robert presented the girls with a potted version of the truth. Rosamund's long nose twitched with scepticism but Bunny looked hopeful, willing to be convinced.

'Doesn't he look well?' she had said as they watched him walk up the path.

And indeed he did. He felt well, too. Since that day a fortnight earlier when he had finally confronted Martina, he had found a new confidence and sense of capability growing within him.

Nothing had been said since, but between husband and wife there was a new understanding. They were gentle with one another though watchful. Robert found that once he had told Martina what he knew, he had begun to feel quite differently about her. He was not angry or disgusted; what he felt towards her now was what he felt towards Louisa – a sense of responsibility.

And he was delighted to take it on board. His shoulders were broad enough, his energy unbounded. It was as if he had recovered from some long disease and was suddenly physically capable of a range of demanding tasks.

Today, although Martina did not know it, Robert had begun his first step in the campaign. He had decided that the rehabilitation of Martina must be a combined effort by those who loved her. It was a task he could embark on alone but he believed that Martina would benefit from the concern of all her family. Now, looking at the engaged and serious expressions on the faces of his sisters, he felt he had made the right decision.

Rosamund grappled to understand. 'Explain it again, Robert.

Martina is the one who is ill but you are the one who ended up drinking too much.'

'I know it's hard to understand. I couldn't face up to the fact that she was ill – it was easier to have another glass of whiskey. But alcohol was never the problem.'

The sisters smiled at one another; they had never believed that it was.

'And once I admitted to myself that she was the problem, I knew I could cope. Actually, it was Lou who made me see how things really stood.'

'Does Martina know she's ill?'

'I think so. Oh yes, I'm sure she does now.'

'So the roles are more or less reversed?'

'I still have to persuade Martina to see a psychiatrist and that may not be too easy – you know the sort of ideas people have about psychiatrists.'

Rosamund squared her shoulders, ready for action. 'So how can we help, Robert?'

'Just the fact that you know is a start and that I can count on you.'

'I should jolly well think so – what are families for?'

Bunny patted his hand. 'You have our support. Anything we can do, just ask us. Perhaps Martina would like to come down – I mean, when she's at the convalescent stage? We could teach her to throw pots. It's wonderfully therapeutic, even if you don't have any talent.'

The girls sat back and looked at their handsome brother. It was like old times – the Persses pulling together against the world. They felt vindicated, for they had never believed in Robert's alcoholism: Persses drank, of course, and drank too much on occasion, but they didn't succumb to it – that was for lesser breeds.

On their rare visits to St Patrick's they had been puzzled, and a teeny bit annoyed with Martina for putting him there. With Robert's explanation, everything fell into place.

Martina must be brought back to health – as Robert's wife

and Lou's mother, that went without saying. The girls were determined to pull their weight, make whatever sacrifices were necessary, even to the point of setting aside their commitments and putting their careers in cold storage – for a certain length of time, at any rate.

They began to think of ways in which they might help. Bunny, who had suffered her own dark night of the soul when Billy Blood-Bermingham had walked away laughing and snorting with derision at the idea of a tryst, thought that talking might help. She could see herself winning Martina's confidence, drawing her aside when the others had gone to bed, indulging in girlish exchanges over hot milk on long evenings.

Rosamund's remedy was radically different – *corpus sana* was the key: long walks, plenty of fresh vegetables, and cut down on red meat which every enlightened person now knew to be the cause of most of man's problems from infertility to baldness.

The girls could be depended on to row in.

'Would you like to see the photograph that Lou just sent?' Robert opened his jacket and took out his wallet. 'Isn't she a funny girl – she had it taken specially in case we were fretting.'

'She looks well.'

'She's got the Persse smile.'

Robert finished the last of his whiskey and stood up.

'I must be off.'

Bunny had presented him with the whiskey when he arrived, offering him no choice, brooking no argument. He had enjoyed the drink, but had no desire for another. He knew himself to be well, as he hadn't been for years. More importantly, he knew that he had both the energy and commitment to come to the aid of his wife. A union which had produced something as lovely and functioning as the girl whose face now smiled up at him deserved to be saved.

And besides, he loved her mother.

'I'll be in touch then, and I'll keep you posted.'

The girls waved him goodbye, standing in the doorway until the red tail lights of his car had disappeared into the gloom.

In the suburbs of Dublin, about two miles from their house on the square, Martina and Robert passed one another, their cars going in opposite directions.

They did not see each other, both intent on their missions: Robert to save Martina, Martina to find and rescue something from the past.

If they had noticed one another, if Robert had honked his horn as they passed, Martina might have waved; she certainly wouldn't have stopped. Her thoughts were busy elsewhere, as they had been since that moment she had fled, running as she so often did *in extremis* to the top of her tall house. There she had flung herself against a window, to stand looking down at the garden. She didn't, however, see the lawn, lumpy with new growth, the dark herbaceous border, the swards of early bulbs under the trees. Instead, there was a tiny square of grass, a gate painted bright blue and a low stone wall. Behind, a cottage stood with its door open. The sun shone hotly and seven-year-old Martina stood in the sunshine, watching the bees on the rose bush. It was a tall bush, taller than Martina, covered in white flowers. The scent coming from them filled the still air, spicy, tickling her nostrils, causing her to sneeze. On the doorstep Granda sat smoking his pipe, and inside, in the dark cave of the house, Granny could be heard banging pots around on the range while Mother sang.

With a pang at her heart, the adult Martina realized that her mother would then have been some fifteen years younger than she herself was today.

The little girl became irritated with the preoccupation of the bees, their total absorption in their task. She clapped her hands, shouted at them, but they continued their golden labours. Taking a handkerchief from her pocket she spread it on the rose bush and waited for a bee to land. As soon as it did, she gathered the corners of the material, imprisoning the insect. She began to dance across to her grandfather, handkerchief held aloft. Suddenly, the bee had had enough. Martina dropped the handkerchief and screamed.

Mother and grandmother came running; Granda threw down his pipe. Seven-year-old Martina was petted, she was hugged; her hair was smoothed with loving hands. The sting was removed and blue stuff was put on the thumb to soothe it. When Auntie Rose returned home on her bicycle, she was dispatched back to the village with a billycan to get a block of ice-cream.

It was an incident perfectly recalled. Mother had worn a spotted dress – a shower-of-hail – short-sleeved and covered by a floral apron. Granny, as usual, had been in black, her legs, even in that heat, encased in lisle stockings. Granda's moustache drooped and was stained yellow at the edges; under his eyes grew strange, red nodules. On the back carrier of Auntie Rose's bike her pink cardigan was folded and neatly secured. When the ice-cream arrived, it had been cut into chunks with the bread knife, served in blue glass bowls and sprinkled with raspberry cordial.

No pleasure since had surpassed the delights of that bowl of ice-cream, and none could be so clearly recalled. 'Have more,' they said, kissing her, watching her as she closed her eyes and savoured the shocking cold, the sharpish raspberry flavour, the creamy aftertaste. 'Have more – more. There's plenty in Duignan's shop and Granda is made of money.'

The vision had faded with the spring sunshine and in the attic Martina had shivered. But as she descended to the basement to cook Robert's supper, her thoughts were still absent. She hardly noticed him as he hovered around the kitchen, being helpful.

That evening, however, he could not be ignored. His well-being filled the house. It overflowed from the armchair where he sat and came bounding across the room so that Martina had to put up a hand to fend it off as one would a large and foolish puppy.

There was nothing mean or selfish in it. It wanted to embrace her; it demanded that she let go, leave it all to a newly-well and capable husband. As she had once, a thousand years ago when she was young.

That was impossible, Martina knew, although she could not as yet sit down and face what it was that she denied with such vehemence. Her thoughts were full of Auntie Rose: she must be confronted; that's where Martina's occupation must lie. That other problem which hovered at the edge of her mind, like an irritating speck in the corner of one's eye, that was something she would tackle later.

'Give me time,' she had said to Robert. 'Later . . . I must have time.'

'Of course. We have all the time in the world.'

Martina and Robert had often gone on holidays to the West of Ireland but it was years since she had travelled this particular route, stopping well short of the coast in a prosperous, inland part of County Galway. It was a place that had changed little since her grandmother's time for, whereas tourism had brought modernity to the coast, this area had few visitors and lived a placid, self-satisfied sort of life. Martina, nervous of how Rose would receive her, for she had not kept in touch over the years, remembered the sense of superiority she had enjoyed on summer holidays, a city child lording it over the yokels.

She passed the road which would lead down to her grandparents' old house and headed for the village where Rose now lived. She had married a publican and still lived over the pub with her older son and his family.

Martina was surprised by the number of landmarks she was beginning to recognize. There was the graveyard with its broken wall, the green-painted pump which hadn't worked even thirty years ago; Murtagh's garage, still an eyesore. She remembered that there had been some sort of scandal attached to the Murtagh family but she couldn't remember what it was.

The village itself was pretty, radiating outwards from a triangular green into three almost intact Georgian terraces. Although businesses were carried on in many of the ground floors, the houses were little disturbed and rose above the shops in pleasing order and simplicity.

Martina's eyes rested with pleasure on the arched entrances to old mews, the shallow granite steps leading to fine doorways. Perhaps this was where her love of the classical had sprung from; perhaps the symmetry of these buildings had been imprinted on her mind as she had walked around these little streets, her hand held in a loving clasp.

She sighed with the realization that the house on the square was no longer her home. Whatever happened now, she could not see herself living there in a year's time.

Rose cocked a quizzical eyebrow.

'It's never – it's not – it's Martina! Where did you come from? And you haven't changed a bit – I'd know you if I met you in the middle of O'Connell Street above in Dublin. Come in, love, come in and join the party.'

Although she had heard nothing on the doorstep, Martina now realized that there were party sounds coming down the stairs: the hubbub of voices and a piano being played.

'I don't want to interrupt anything.'

'As if you could – my own flesh and blood. The boys are off to Cheltenham in the morning and we're having a bit of a hooley before they go. This is terrible racing country, Martina – half the town'll be gone tomorrow. Terry likes us to have a bit of a sing-song here – to wish them good luck. Not that they ever win anything.'

She laughed, shoving Martina up the stairs in front of her.

Martina would not have recognized her cousins: she remembered them as gawky youths, for they were some years younger than she. Now they stood to greet her, stocky men, their broad faces creasing in smiles, shy but friendly.

'How're you doing?' they inquired, pumping her hand in turn. 'What are you having to drink?'

Rose shoved them out of the way.

'Will you give the girl a chance. Come over here with me and

123

let me look at you. Do you know what it is – you haven't changed a bit. You're still the lovely girl you always were.'

The cousins' wives gathered round, smart in bright, tight trouser suits and high-heeled boots. Rose smiled fondly at them and told them to go and make fresh tea.

'And how's your man – Robert, wasn't that his name?'

Around the walls the guests sat, straight-backed on kitchen chairs, looking as they might in doctors' waiting rooms except for the glasses in their hands. Martina sank back on to the leather-covered settee, obviously the seat of honour.

'I'm that glad to see you, Martina,' said Rose, taking her hand. 'I couldn't be more delighted if I'd won the big prize in the Lottery.'

Martina took a sandwich and a cup of tea; despite her protests, a tumbler of whiskey was waiting, already poured at her elbow. She looked around her: the room was not unlike Bridie's front room except on a larger and more opulent scale. Burnished brass was massed round the fire place; souvenirs from Majorca and Yugoslavia and the Algarve crowded the tops of the shiny reproduction furniture; the windows were double-glazed and in front of them the pale-blue curtains fell in generous folds right down to the ground.

Watching her niece's eyes move round the room, Rose smiled with innocent pleasure.

'I always said I'd have a nice room, as nice as your Mammy's, God be good to her. None of the grandchildren are allowed in here, you know; Granny keeps the key in her handbag – it's the only way I could keep it nice.'

Martina slept that night between floral Easi-care sheets under a pink candlewick bedspread. The party had continued on until midnight, when Rose had dismissed the revellers saying that they all had to be up for early Mass in the morning.

'They laugh at me,' she had told Martina as she accompanied her upstairs to bed. 'They say I'm very old fashioned. But I make them go to the sacraments before they get on a plane – I mean, you never know what's going to happen once you get up there.' She kissed Martina goodnight. 'And tell me, now – did you enjoy the party?'

Enjoy was not the appropriate word. Martina knew that her trip had not been a waste of time and that the evening would have taught her something if she could understand its significance and her own complex reaction to it.

This was her world, the world of her people. She had not belonged to it for many years but she had recognized it instantly as one does with a shock a sudden whiff of some essence from one's childhood. For many years she had been *déclassé*, *déraciné* even, belonging nowhere, part of no community. For her, social intercourse had become like those childhood music lessons which she had neither enjoyed nor understood.

Bridie would have enjoyed tonight's party; she would have fitted in effortlessly. It was this acceptance, even pleasure in who she was that had so infuriated her daughter, that had ultimately led to Martina's betrayal of her.

Now Martina wondered why she had made such a fuss. Bridie's preference for sweet sherry was hardly a crime, any more than was Rose's pride in her over-furnished front room. Her cousins' view of the world was as valid as any and more attractive than most. And was it more atavistic of Rose to want her sons shrived before they boarded the plane than of Charlotte to want *her* son to treasure and pass on his great grandfather's war medals?

Martina had learned a concomitant truth tonight – she could not go back. She was of these people but she was different: experiences had marked her out, changed her; or perhaps she had been born with a few odd chromosomes. And she knew also that, for all her warm feelings of returning, if she did try to live here among them, as herself, they would turn their backs on her as surely as they had welcomed her tonight. The price of acceptance was orthodoxy and Martina was now too alloyed to return to that.

In the morning she rose and went to Mass with her family. Then, refusing the offer of breakfast, she set out for Dublin. As she drove through the calm, already green countryside, she felt that some area of muddle and guilt had been resolved – her betrayal of Bridie.

In the past, looking at a gathering of the Persses, listening to them talk their language and sign their secret signs, Martina had often sighed and said to herself: If only . . . She had never allowed herself to complete the phrase but she knew that what she had been wishing for was that the same sort of continuum she had witnessed among her in-laws could have been shared by herself and Bridie. It had seemed so rich, so positive, so resoundingly strong, and Charlotte, its beneficiary, so blessed by comparison with poor Bridie.

Crossing over the bridge at Shannon Harbour, Martina had stopped the car and got out. She had looked down at the river, seeing the uneven indentation of its banks. Beyond, towards Offaly, some fields still bore the marks of its flood water, while on the opposite bank the earth seemed to be making inroads into the watery kingdom, silting up the shallows with a dense and matted growth of reeds. The sky was reflected in the water so that upside-down clouds tumbled over one another in their race to the sea. Above the water swarms of gnats hovered, and along the margins vegetation seemed lush but insubstantial, as if it might at any moment slip from one element to the other.

The flux of this world seemed to the watching Martina like a metaphor for her own. Bridie, herself, Rose and, yes, Louisa – they were all adrift in there, bobbing along, metamorphosing, bleeding and growing, sinking and rising with the current.

Whereas the Persses – they were like the blighted tree she had seen a few miles back, struck by lightning, still standing, unchanging and dead in the living landscape.

Getting back into her car, instead of turning the key in the ignition, she laid her head down on the steering wheel. It wasn't true. Robert was a Persse. Robert . . . Her knuckles grew white as she gripped the wheel, forcing her mind to think of her husband. She could feel it, as if it had a physical reality, slip away from her, dart in one direction and then the other, but she hauled it back. There – Robert – your husband.

She had loved him once.

And I still do.

She might have shouted the words aloud, so resonantly did they echo within her head. And she was surprised by their truth. For years she had ignored this truth or had not acknowledged it to herself or had genuinely not recognized it. Now, as she approached a confrontation which might end in the dissolution of her marriage, she feared that recognition had come too late.

She had made her peace with Bridie, who was now at rest or out there whizzing around in some other galaxy. At least Bridie was out of her daughter's life and her daughter must look to the living whom she had also betrayed.

Martina began to drive, settling down to a steady thirty-five miles an hour. The longer the journey home lasted, the more time she would have to come to some understanding of the past, and in so doing perhaps salvage something of the future.

13

When had she begun to betray Robert? Why had she betrayed him? The early days of their marriage, despite Charlotte, had been happy ones, but, once Louisa was born, Martina had begun to feel vulnerable, even threatened. Reflecting now over the nineteen years, she saw that she had immediately set out to protect herself, to look round to see how she could strike back, although at the time she had not been consciously aware of so doing. The weapon she had chosen, with a sure and destructive instinct, had been sex.

Martina had not come unfettered to sex. She had been brought up in the traditional Catholic world of the fifties, where its horrors were hinted at in school playgrounds and in the dropped voices of one's mother's friends.

In love with Robert, she had, however, embarked on marriage with joy. This joy had found its natural expression in copulation, which Martina had enjoyed without quite knowing what all the fuss was about. She was moved by her husband's handsome body; she had enjoyed stroking and caressing it, but what she had really valued were the interludes of tenderness when it was all over and they lay in one another's arms, sweetly supine. There was a disinterest then in his terms of endearment which she had valued, for it gave them the ring of truth.

He really does love me, then, she would tell herself as she lay awake, feeling with pleasure the tickle of his breath against the back of her neck.

After some months, sex was something she had stopped thinking about; it was part of the happy mesh of marriage – it was just there.

When Louisa was born, mother and daughter had both nearly died. That perfect body was malformed inside, something to do with the positioning of the pelvic bones. Martina, who had gone into a nursing home for what everybody assumed would be a routine birth, was rushed through the night in a screaming ambulance to the nearest maternity hospital.

'The baby cannot be delivered normally,' Robert was told. 'We must perform a section immediately if we are to save it. And the mother is in some distress at this stage, too.'

Robert had waited, pacing the sweating linoleum of the hospital corridor. Beyond the brown painted doors, his future was being decided.

When a green-gowned figure emerged and flitted past, he ran after it, crying, 'Save my wife. It doesn't matter about the baby but you must save Martina.'

The figure had turned. 'For goodness sake, Mr Persse, will you stop fussing. Everything is under control – this is all fairly routine here, you know. Your wife is fine.'

But Robert was never to believe that again. Martina had entered the nursing home a healthy young animal and suddenly her life was in danger. For ever after, her fragility was fixed in his mind.

When he saw her next morning, the strain showing around the lovely mouth despite the happiness in the eyes, he determined that this was one danger at least she need never again be exposed to.

The job was done discreetly, without fuss or bother. Martina was told when it was all over. She had looked at her husband uncomprehendingly. 'But why did you have it done? I could have had more babies – once they knew I'd simply have had the others by Caesarian, too. I'm only twenty-three, Robert.'

'We're a family now, Martina: we have our baby, our darling daughter. I don't want you going through this again. I won't have you cut open.'

Seeing the love on his face, the features exposed and vulnerable, her bewilderment and anger had turned to guilt. It was her fault;

129

if she had been normal like other women, she could have borne many children, boys and girls. As an only child herself, she had always looked wistfully at the large families around her and had often vowed that her children would enjoy the sort of childhood which her isolation had denied her.

Charlotte's first visit to the hospital had compounded Martina's feelings of guilt. 'How are you, my dear?' she had asked, thrusting a wilting potted primula towards her chest and, before Martina had time to answer, she had turned and picked up the baby. 'Well, my angel, my precious, what a beauty you are. And they tell me you are going to be all on your own? Never mind, Grandma will look after you and leave you all her money when she dies. Then you'll be an heiress and, when you get married, your husband can change his name to Persse – it's happened before.'

She turned to beam at Martina. 'Nobody could mistake her for anything but a Persse – could they? She looks exactly like Bunny when Bunny was this age.'

It was only when she was leaving that she suddenly remembered herself and returned from the door to pat Martina's hand. 'Clever girl. We must look after you and see that you get well soon. No running around from now on, with your new responsibilities.'

Martina stared after her as the door swung closed. What had she done? She placed both hands on her stomach to stop her sobs tearing at the wound. In its crib, the baby too had begun to whimper. Martina stared across at it.

She had destroyed her autonomy; she had ensnared herself, shackled herself for life to this Persse baby.

Manoeuvring herself out of the high hospital bed, she picked her way to the baby's crib. She looked at her daughter, the scowling red face split in two, the upper half disappearing into the lank black fringe.

They would take her over and discard the clucking hen now that she had done her work. They might even look round for a pot in which to chuck the hen, for she would hatch no more chicks, not Persse ones, at any rate.

The baby began to howl. A nurse came in and helped Martina back to bed and placed the baby at her breast. As the little face began to snuffle round for the nipple, Martina could sense its anxiety, its tiny, helpless hands, like feathers beating against her. She gathered the baby closer to her, literally shaking with the surge of emotion which welled up from her bruised and aching body. She made, then, a secret pact with Louisa. She would protect her and watch over her but she would see to it that she grew up free. The Persses wouldn't own her; her mother wouldn't own her. She would be strong and invulnerable and never suffer as foolish Martina had suffered. She would be her own woman.

Martina recovered quickly from her operation and Louisa proved a model baby. Her parents marvelled at her placidity but the district nurse, when she came to visit, said that it was only natural.

'She's had a great start, you know. No long journey down the birth canal, no fighting to get into the world nor nasty forceps. She was just lifted out, easy as pie – no wonder she's smiling.'

It seemed to Martina that she, too, was happy. She had forgotten about Robert's vasectomy, or at least put it to the back of her mind, and, with Louisa occupying all her time, she didn't worry about the future. She would have said that things were back as they had been, only with the added pleasure of little Lou. However, when Louisa was about two months old and Robert, laughing, had told her that he was getting desperate and how about a kiss and a cuddle, Martina discovered a new problem. She found that she was filled with a distaste at the idea of sex – almost amounting to nausea. She gritted her teeth, admonished herself to be sensible but as she felt Robert's hand on her breast, smelled his smell, she found herself gagging.

'I'm sorry, Robert, it's just too soon. You'll have to give me more time.'

He was understanding and gentle, apologizing for rushing her.

Time changed nothing: three months later her reactions were the same and Martina knew she was in trouble.

Robert's forbearance was exemplary but it did nothing to assuage the panic which now swept over Martina. She viewed her husband suddenly with a mixture of fear and dislike. She was sure that he would leave her and, much worse, take Louisa with him. What if he claimed custody? She could not fight an army of Persses and no judge would find in favour of a woman who denied a good and loving husband his connubial rights. At night she dreamt of Louisa being taken from her; in the daytime she sat by her cot, fearful of leaving the baby alone for five minutes in case she was whisked away. It was purely by chance that she found a solution to her problem.

She had not been sleeping well and had taken to reading late into the night; she had also reached the stage where sleep was impossible unless Robert was already snoring beside her. One night, finding herself without her usual thriller, she had gone to bed with a romance. She hadn't read this sort of thing since her teenage years and she turned to it now with no great enthusiasm, but, as she made her way through the predictable story, she found herself surprised by her reactions. The heroine of the tale was pure, according to the convention; the man she loved so passionately kissed her on the lips; she felt his strong arms crush her to him, at which point the novelist dropped a discretionary veil. Martina read, noting with one part of her mind the execrable writing, but becoming more interested in the series of signals coming from her body, all of them suggesting sexual arousal.

When Robert, who had been out dining with a client, finally got into bed, he was surprised and gratified by what he found.

Martina was intrigued. She began to experiment. She got her hands on a variety of pornography, from the hard to the soft, but it all left her unmoved; it was old-fashioned romance which excited her.

It began to work like a drug. If she didn't read the relevant chapters, she would find herself unable to respond to Robert

132

and all her old feelings of distaste would return. On the other hand, the more she read the more stimulated she became and the more erotic her fantasies. She suddenly found her head filled with ideas whose genesis was a mystery; certainly, they bore no relation to the chaste romances she had been feeding herself. Now she found she wanted to make love and was aggressive, immodest in her demands for pleasure. She would read for an hour or two, then rise, go to the bathroom, strip off her nightdress and stand in front of the mirror. She would look at her body, admire it, touch it, then stride back to the bedroom, naked.

In the morning, when she thought of her behaviour the night before, she would be overcome by shame, but she'd remind herself that it was necessary, a ploy to keep Robert and thus Louisa. She found, too, that she had begun to blame Robert for her behaviour. As he lay beside her afterwards, abject in his gratitude, she would turn her back on him in contempt, knowing that what had passed between them was not an act of love, not on her part, and that she was all the stronger for this.

All this Martina now faced as she drove slowly towards Dublin. She believed that she understood her behaviour a little better and, as she followed the thread backwards through the maze of the past, she came up against a startling revelation – a recognition of her own frigidity. She could imagine Robert's derision at such a notion, see him producing night after night of evidence to refute it, but the more she probed, the surer she became.

The pattern of her behaviour had been engendered by accident, and initially it was out of fear that she had seized upon what the romances offered. Her contempt for Robert, however, was something separate – she despised him because he loved her and expressed this love through sex. She could become aroused only through romance, the usual feminine reaction of wanting to make love solely to whomever one was in love with. Well, she had turned that notion on its head with a vengeance, either because she had no longer believed in Robert's love for her or because her love for him had been destroyed by exposure to the Persse family. Whatever the reason, she had ended up finding

133

her stimulation in romantic trash instead of in her husband, and she had wreaked vengeance on him by deliberately indulging in acts of mechanical sex, despising him the meanwhile for his tenderness.

The marriage must have been bleeding internally for years. She had injured herself as surely as she had injured Robert. The problem was, she didn't know now if she could do anything about it.

She stopped the car again, this time pulling in to a lay-by, one of those sordid little resting bays that litter Irish roads. She turned off the ignition, pulled on the handbrake and deliberately set herself to examine her attitude to sex.

If she were honest with herself, she would admit that it appalled her: the raw and ugly look of private parts, the horrid feel of pubic hair, so different from the hair on one's head; the clumsiness of two panting, straining bodies; the smell, the mess. Was God having a laugh at their expense? How differently He arranged things for the lesser orders of His creation: she considered the elegance of fish, the economy of birds. By comparison, the unseemly thrashing around of man and woman seemed an absurdity.

Then, logically, she should walk away: Lou was fledged. And Robert – Robert? She was not done yet; there was reparation yet to be made for her sins of omission. But how?

She looked around her. From the road she could hear the hum of traffic but the cars and lorries that whizzed by were obscured by high hedges. The ground in front of her was strewn with tins and broken bottles. Shreds of coloured plastic waved in the breeze like Buddhist emblems, caught on the thorns of the hedges.

She could die here – it would be so easy. She would get her rug from the back seat, wrap it round her, slit her wrists with the silver fruit knife on her key-ring, a birthday present from Robert. Then she would lie down under the hedge and wait for unconsciousness to overtake her. By the time the tourists returned she would have rotted down, adding humus to the soil. Wrapped in her woollen blanket, it would be an act of perfect ecological responsibility. Unlike the plastic, no bits of her would remain fluttering in the breeze to despoil the countryside. Greenpeace might adopt her as their first saint.

It was so infinitely desirable, so right, this picture of her sinking back into the boggy earth whence her ancestors had sprung. And so much more aesthetic than being dumped in a neatly dug hole of designated dimensions, every square inch around you requisitioned by the families of the other stiffs.

Then the unimaginable luxury of non-being. No pain, no foolish hopes, no dreadful tomorrows. No blame, no shame.

A bird with something in its mouth caught Martina's attention as it flew past the windscreen. It had come this way before – twice, she thought. Nest building in the hedge opposite, which would soon have grown dense with new buds.

She turned on the ignition and nosed her way once more into the traffic. All living things had their season and she was still green and full of sap. Not in years but certainly in what remained to be done. She had promises to keep.

'And miles to go before I sleep,' she said aloud and turned on the car radio.

14

The house on the square already looked unloved. The heavy brass door knocker was dull and unpolished; the window glass was smeared. Upstairs in the drawing-room the curtains hung awry.

Louisa sat, as she had on so many occasions, looking down on the square, nose flattened against the glass. She was waiting for Martina to come home, which she should do at any minute now according to the note she had left on the kitchen table.

Louisa's return had been undertaken on impulse. Lying on her hostel bed in London, she had thought: What am I doing here? God knows what's going on in Dublin, what's happening to Dad.

She had stuffed her few clothes into a canvas bag and was on her way to Euston without a backward glance.

Louisa was determined to travel light through life. She had assessed London coolly, taking its huge size and bustle in her stride. She was not fazed by it and she marched through the Underground in her sturdy boots, stood on moving staircases with her arms folded, elbowed her way through the West End streets as if she had been born there. She left it now without compunction, as she would one day leave it more permanently to head off to Paris or New York, but never, unlike today, back to Dublin. She had to go back to sort things out; if necessary, to rescue Robert and take him back with her. After that Dublin was *finito*, the slate wiped clean. She had no intention of hanging around feeling all churned up inside – she had a life to be lived.

A surprise awaited her. The first thing she noticed as she let herself in by the area door was the level of heat; in her memory the thermostat had never been turned up so extravagantly high. Then, as she made her way down the corridor, she saw that the house, while not actually dirty, did have a scuffed appearance.

Robert was in the kitchen, shredding cabbage. In front of him was a glass of white wine and an open book into which he was peering.

He enveloped her in a soggy embrace. 'You're just in time for dinner. Prawns Cantonese style for one but I've loads of prawns. Start shelling.'

He poured her a glass of wine and drew out a stool for her. She could see that he was slightly absent-minded, his attention fixed on the prawns. As she sipped her wine, she noticed also his altered mien: there was a carelessness in the set of his shoulders and his face seemed blank without its customery puckers. With a shock she thought: He's happy.

'Where is Mother?'

'She's gone to visit Rose – you remember your Aunt Rose?'

They shared a bottle of wine and then sat down together in front of the study fire, leaving the washing up till the morning.

'I'm glad you've come, Lou – I was going to write and ask you to.'

'There's really no reason for me to hang around London – I'm not actually starting at college until the autumn, you know. And I was worried about you. I mean, I got you out of the hospital and then sort of abandoned you. But you look well.'

'I'm fine – even better, now that you're home. We must talk.' Robert caught her hand. 'We have a lot to discuss and we have wasted so much time. Our lives could have been so different if only I'd realized sooner what I do now.'

The plausibility of what he said lay in Louisa's desire to believe. She recognized the sham of her indifference, despite all the effort that had gone into it as she listened to Robert explain how Martina had always loved her.

'She's been ill for years; that's what I should have recognized sooner. She needs psychiatric help.'

'What's wrong with her?'

'I'm not a psychiatrist but you can see that she's not – she's never been – '

'Normal?'

'Happy – for years. Maybe it was my fault. I never faced her with it; I used to pretend to myself that nothing was wrong. I think I never fully convinced myself that she was all right – there was always a worry at the back of my mind. And her coldness towards you, Lou, when she adores you – that's all part of it.'

'I wonder.'

'No, listen. You should have seen her when you were a baby, she wouldn't leave your side for a second. And she talked to you all the time, telling you how beautiful you were, how much she loved you. I'd see her face when she was looking down at you. Transformed. You don't just turn off love like that. For some reason she couldn't express it any more. Oh, there are other things, too, Lou, that I'll tell you about some day. You've got to help me, Lou – we've got to convince her to go and see someone.'

'If you think – '

'I do. As I said, the pity is I didn't do it years ago, it would have saved you both so much pain.'

'And you.'

'I had my whiskey, until it got out of hand. And I had the two of you, more than most men get in a lifetime.'

Louisa felt the barriers coming down around her heart. Memory waves began to swamp her so that she was afloat on the past. She could feel again the intensity of her love for her mother as she looked up into her beautiful face. At school, when she read poems about the fair beloved, she had always thought of Martina, whose fairness seemed all the more remarkable among the dark-haired Persses.

And her calmness, her gentleness, the low musicality of her voice. The love had been tinged with awe, for there was always a reserve around Martina which warned you, even her daughter, not to presume.

When the six-year-old Louisa used to be asked, 'What do you want to be when you grow up?' she would answer truthfully, 'I want to be like Mummy.'

Schoolfriends had envied her this paragon who didn't scream like other mothers or tell you to buzz off out of the way. Louisa's queries were patiently answered, her body and mind were carefully nurtured. When at first she began to feel unhappy, to sense a niggle of criticism of this perfect mother, she had been confused. What could such a person be accused of? Louisa didn't know, but her heart grew undernourished and the little girl pined.

Now – now she would be modest in her expectations. She blew on the window and then wiped away her breath. She must not think beyond getting Martina better, but it was hard not to feel excited, waiting for this unique reunion.

They had prepared a cold meal, Technicolored delicatessen food, meant to reassure Martina, to make her realize that without her this was the sort of fare that would sustain them.

They had met her at the hall door and kissed her, Robert casual and friendly, Louisa, in spite of herself, with yearning. Now they watched her as she ate: watched the pale, thin fingers brush crumbs from the crumpled, pink mouth; watched the eyes veiled in pain; watched and waited and held their breaths.

'Did you find Rose well?'

'Yes. Oh yes.'

'You must have noticed a lot of changes?'

'Indeed.'

She seemed to want to say more but couldn't find the words.

'Let's go out somewhere – it's a terrific evening.'

It was a sad little outing. They went to the Phoenix Park, chosen by Robert because of its association with happier days. When Lou was small they used to come here on fine weekends, when it had seemed like a rural paradise on their doorsteps. They would watch the polo for a bit, then wander off in search of the herds of grazing deer. There were trees for Lou to climb, slopes for her to roll down, hidden pockets of wilderness for them all to explore.

Now they sat on a bench and looked at its level acres with the smoky mountains beyond. The giant concrete cross erected to mark the Papal visit dwarfed everything around it so that the group of youths lolling at its base looked like so many ragged little puppets, waiting for the puppet master to arrive.

'Not as warm as I thought,' said Robert. 'Shall we walk on?'

They wandered more than walked, moving without direction. Conversation came in scraps, taken up then dropped; the shadows of former outings settled round them like fog. Robert didn't know whether or not it was a good thing that Martina now looked out on the world with quiet sadness, that the awful brightness which she had carried round with her for years had at last been dropped, but he could feel her mood encompassing the three of them. Yesterday Louisa and he had hatched plans with such vitality; today that vitality seemed an affront to this fragile, flaccid creature.

The old Martina would not return. This sad woman who looked at them with too much pity was hard to accept.

He made a final effort. 'Look, you two, over there – isn't that Lou's tree?'

But as he began to stride towards it, Louisa put out her hand.

'Don't, Daddy, please. Let's go and have a drink.'

However, the pub did nothing to lessen their nervousness, the noise and chatter merely emphasizing their isolation. Even the novelty of a newly-adult daughter sitting on a high stool could not dissipate the sense of impending calamity. Without consultation they emptied their glasses and slid from the counter, moving one after the other towards the door.

Louisa fled to her bedroom.

'Tomorrow,' she told herself, 'everything will be all right. When she's slept, when they've spent a night together, things will look quite different.'

Upstairs, her parents stood looking out on the garden, fearful of turning back towards the room when they must begin talking.

140

Robert put an arm around his wife's shoulder, then withdrew it as he felt her muscles stiffen.

'I'm sorry.'

'Martina – it's natural. Come and sit down.'

He led her across to her seat, underneath the lamp.

'We must talk, Martina.'

She felt herself beginning to tremble.

'For the first time in our lives we must be honest with one another – everything out in the open. Everything up front, as Lou would say.'

She acknowledged this with a wan smile.

'It's our only hope. Listen, darling – ' She flinched. ' – I've been talking to Dr Morgan – no, I haven't told him anything specific. I know I used to laugh at him but he's a competent doctor; I believe he could help us. He suggested family therapy.'

'Oh, family therapy, I don't know – '

'Don't say no, Martina, think about it. We can't go back; there's no use pretending that certain things haven't happened. What you did – no, don't turn away, Martina, I'm not accusing you, but you need help.'

Martina felt as if she might drown. The shame rose and engulfed her; the blood flooded through her arteries so she knew that the very whites of her eyes must have blushed crimson.

'We must have truth, honesty. That's the only way our marriage can survive. I must try to discover how I failed you, how I drove you to such a thing.'

'It wasn't anything to do with you.'

'Yes it was. You made me happy.'

Martina looked at her husband. She had got out of the habit of looking at him and now she was surprised to find that he was still an attractive man. Not much different from the one she had fallen in love with: thinner, more worn, creased here and there.

She could try; she could begin by saying – She closed her eyes but she could still see him. He was a stranger, yet through the osmosis of marriage he had become part of her. To cut herself off now would mean amputation – she would emerge deformed.

She must try. Maybe Dr Morgan. Or just talking, if she could only once begin.

'You've been under a strain for years – I knew it but I didn't recognize it. And because I was happy, I fooled myself into believing that you were too. And you never wept or shouted, Martina. In our family, whenever anything was wrong, nobody would be left in any doubt about it. I just didn't recognize your gentler responses. But it's not too late to start – is it?'

Yes, yes, a hundred years too late.

'We love one another – you do still love me, Martina? And there's darling Lou. We made her, Martina, and she is perfection. We'll keep the house or sell it, whatever you wish. And we don't have to stay in Dublin – we could go abroad. Just so's we stay together.'

The seductiveness of the vision gave her pause. Maybe. Robert might forget; they might be able to go on without going back over everything. If they could live abroad, if there were nothing to remind them, nothing rising up reeking of associations. The other course, Robert's suggestion, was unthinkable.

'We must give it a try, Martina. I know we can do it. You know, I haven't felt like this for years.'

Most of the drawing-room lay in shadow. The single lamp which shone down on Martina's head caught Robert also in its refracted rays as he stood, leaning against the mantelpiece. His head thrown back, his features varnished by the light, he seemed to Martina a *quattrocento* figure: beautiful, dominant and yet impotent.

She rose and stretched up her arms to embrace him. 'There,' she said, smoothing down his hair.

Robert felt the cold rising in his chest as air rushed in to fill the space created by a contracting heart. This was no reconciliatory embrace which Martina offered him. This, he could smell it in the air, was a valediction.

15

My dear ones,

I hope by now you have received my postcards and that you are at least not worried about me. You will know that I am safe and that I am gone, if not for ever, at least for a very long time. I thought if I wrote a letter before now that you might burn it unread and I did want you to understand, in so far as you can, what my motives were for leaving. I do not ask for forgiveness.

I can see quite clearly now how much I love you and will always love you. Love is not necessarily what keeps a family together, however – there are other considerations.

As you see from the address, I am living in Spain. When I left Dublin, I went straight to London – the classic escape route. I never intended to stay there, however, because I felt it was Louisa's city. I suppose you would consider this absurd, in such a huge city, but I had a sort of superstitious feeling that I might blight your life even further, Lou, by hanging around breathing your air. Besides, I only had a limited amount of money and I couldn't see myself getting work there. To be truthful, I couldn't see myself getting work anywhere – this was something I had never thought about in Dublin in my panic to get away.

Then, just as I was getting worried about the amount of money I had left, I was passing by Marks & Spencer in Oxford Street one Friday evening when this woman rushed up to me and said, 'Aren't you Martina O'Donnell?'

143

I was amazed – in the middle of London! And no one had called me O'Donnell for a long time. It turned out that she was a girl I went to school with, Joan Kavanagh, although I would never have recognized her. She was laden down with parcels and surrounded by black-eyed children, and she told me that she was over from Madrid on a shopping trip. I've learned since coming here that Spaniards, even the wealthy ones, do this quite a lot – they love the M. & S. woollies and they are so much cheaper than inferior quality over here. Joan had gone to Spain soon after leaving school and she had married a Spaniard. I was very pleased to see her – I hadn't realized until then how lonely I'd been – and I persuaded them all to come round to my bedsit, even though I couldn't offer them much.

We squeezed into my little room and Joan was given the only armchair. She seemed to me to have aged a great deal and she was quite fat. But the children were swarming all over her and kissing her and calling her Mami. One girl was about your age, Lou, with short hair just like yours, and, when I saw her stroking her mother's arm, I just couldn't help it, I started to cry.

Then of course, the whole story came out – well, not the true version. I just told her that my marriage had broken up and that I was living in London with no job prospects and very little money. She was very sympathetic, and after a while she came up with a plan: I should go back to Spain with her and I would soon find a position teaching English. It didn't seem very likely to me but she said she had connections as she used to do that sort of thing before the children arrived. Anyway, I had nothing to lose, so I pawned my engagement ring (I'm enclosing the ticket for you, Lou) and bought a one-way ticket to Madrid.

Joan was very kind to me – I can never repay her. I stayed with her until I got a position, which was quite easy really. I've had to pretend that I'm a *viuda* (widow) down on her luck, as it's more respectable, but Joan's recommendation and the fact that I was educated by the Loreto nuns were a help in establishing my credentials. My age, too, has worked in my favour, odd though that may seem – I'm considered less flighty than a young girl would be.

It's a strange life, mainly because of my age. There are plenty of *señoritas* teaching English over here but they're all about your age, Lou. I don't socialize with them and the only person I see apart from the family is Joan, and that's not very often, as she lives out in the suburbs.

My family consists of a mother and father, two daughters, eighteen and twenty-one, and a ten-year-old son, Julio. The latter is my pupil. I teach him English two hours a day and I supervise his homework. I also sew for the girls, who are students but live like duchesses, and I get paid extra for that. I manage to save quite a lot as I have nothing to spend my money on. If I stay two years, the family will pay my fare back to London.

We live in the Castellana, a smart part of the city, quite near the centre. Madrid is a very interesting city – terrible sprawling suburbs but a small intact centre. On one level it seems like a modern, European metropolis and then you come across whole chunks that are quite medieval. I like it very much and I do a lot of walking.

The weather just now is lovely, sunny and warm. I'm told it gets unbearably hot in July but by then we will have gone to the family's summer house in the north. As you can imagine, they are very well off. The grandfather emigrated to Argentina around the turn of the century and made his fortune there. His eldest son – Señor Osca's father – was born there and then the family returned to Asturias – that's where the summer house is today, the old family home. I've learned all this from Maruja, one of the maids who also comes from Asturias and who loves a respectful gossip.

Señor Osca is an engineer but they all live like grandees. There is another ancient maid besides Maruja and they take it in turns to wait on table dressed in black and white uniforms.

145

La comida (lunch) and *la cena* (dinner) are eaten in great solemnity in the dining-room which is furnished in heavy, dark wood. Sometimes I escape and eat earlier with Julio but it is a mark of the esteem in which I am held that I join them for meals. Joan introduced me as Martina Persse-O'Donnell and it is the O'Donnell which impresses over here. It is the family name of the Dukes of Tetúan and Señora Osca is half convinced that I must be some sort of distant Irish connection. Would Charlotte be amused or infuriated?

My Spanish is improving. I practise with Maruja – the other maid is from Andalusia and very hard to understand. The family all like to practise their English – the girls are quite fluent – so I don't get much chance there.

I have a lot of free time. Most afternoons I go to the Prado, which is not very far away. I love it – living with you two over the years, something has obviously rubbed off.

However, there is another reason for visiting the Prado besides aesthetic pleasure – I go for reassurance and to see proof of the redemptive power of love.

You two probably know all about Goya – I knew nothing about him till I came here. The only painting of his I had ever seen was that one in the Beit collection of a rather frowsty Spanish woman. I think it was stolen a few years ago in that big robbery. Anyway, when I discovered Goya in the Prado, I was delighted with him. As you can imagine, I had discovered the early Goya – those lovely scenes of young people picnicking and playing on the banks of the Manzanares. I thought of us, Robert, and the picnics we used to have on the banks of the Liffey in Wicklow – that was the long, hot summer that I was pregnant with you, Lou, and too embarrassed to show myself on a beach.

I moved on to the war paintings: upsetting, yes, but still a positive statement, a reaffirmation of human values against the brutalities of war.

Then came the black paintings. I suppose most people are shocked when they see these for the first time – I was

146

completely devastated. I've since read that most people find it hard to accept that the early pictures and these were painted by the same person. I had no such difficulty – I was looking at my own life writ large.

I thought of that life, its uneventfulness, its bright beginnings and the ugly black thing that it had become. I knew then that Goya's vision was the truth, to which I could add my own insight: the evil at the heart of man could flourish just as vigorously at the domestic hearth as on the battlefields of Europe.

Those grotesque shapes looming down at me from the walls of the Prado reminded me of what I was – of what we all are or have the potential to become.

And then the miracle happened, and it *was* a miracle, for why else would I have looked up at the painting as I trailed away, sure that I would never again return to this museum? But I did look up and I saw a small portrait of a young woman painted with such gentleness and love. It was another Goya, and the miraculous lay in the fact that it came after all the rest, painted by the artist towards the end of his life when he was in his eighties.

She was so real, her eyes so full of happiness and joy, that I sat down and wept tears of gratitude to that old man, imagining the arthritic hands applying the brush strokes, each one proclaiming that goodness could exist and might perhaps ultimately conquer. My guide book told me she was a milkmaid.

The sun plays the sort of role in Spanish life that the rain does in Irish. One of the main squares of the city is called Puerta del Sol – the gate of the sun. Even in winter, it shines practically every day. And the light is so bright after Ireland where it now seems to me we live in perpetual twilight. Here, they have to protect themselves against the fierceness of the sun – streets are built to exclude it, shutters are shut against it. It is less enervating than our perpetual drizzle but also less kind.

But I have received nothing but kindness from the Oscas. On

Sundays, they take me to Mass with them. We go to a different church nearly every week – they are all extraordinary: dark, of course, and filled with the sort of garishly painted statues that make Irish religious art look quite reticent!

Afterwards we go to a café for hot chocolate and *churros* (pieces of fried dough) – delicious. The ladies dress up to the nines – faces and nails painted, gold jewellery jangling. My lack of adornment is approved of and seen as denoting fitting modesty.

I rarely see Joan; as I said, she lives too far away. The life I live among strangers is restful. I sew and study my Spanish grammar and think about the two of you.

It is hard for me to explain and hard for you to understand my motives for walking out. They weren't entirely selfish, and though part of the reason was that I couldn't face the shame (I presume Lou knows all about that now) I also felt that I would do more damage to you both by staying than by getting out.

I never believed in your Dr Morgan, Robert, that he could tell me anything about myself that I didn't already know. I don't believe that you can divide the world into the sane and the mad, just like that. We are all driven mad, at some time, by the pain of life. Those who are not are as the clods of earth.

It is only since I have come to Spain and have been living among strangers that I have been able to bring myself to the point of acknowledging and examining my behaviour. If I had stayed at home, this would have been impossible – shame would have swamped every other impulse and thought. And I wouldn't have been a kind and loving wife and mother: I would have been what I have always been, destructive. What could Dr Morgan have done? Like the TB patients in days gone by, my only hope of a cure is time and isolation. My Spanish family is the equivalent of a sanatorium in Switzerland. And you remember the awful thing about TB? It infects the whole family. I now know that I had been poisoning our family life for years. My only defence is that I didn't know at the time that it was happening. I just hope now that I have got out, that the damage is not irreparable.

You will be all right, Lou – you are young. And now you know that I loved you – you were and are the passion of my life.

You, dear Robert, were the passion of my youth, and still are my dear and beloved husband. Take my love and keep it, both of you.

I know that this is no sort of explanation but it is the best I can do, for the moment. I do hope that some day we may be together again. In the mean time, can we write to one another? Become penpals?! I've only given you a Poste Restante address, just in case you are tempted to come looking for me. You mustn't try to find me or worry about me. My new life is busy and satisfactory and I do have hopes for the future but it will be a slow process. In an emotional sense you two are my life and always will be.

Martina Persse O'Donnell.

PS: I'm sorry this has been such a long, rambling letter. It was harder to write than I had imagined, and hard to end. While I was scribbling, you seemed so close.

M.

On her bench in the Retiro, Martina licked the flap of the envelope and stuck it down. The afternoon sun was hot on her bare arms and she turned her face towards it, indifferent to the damage it would wreak on her pale and ageing skin. How aptly named it was – homesickness. Writing that letter had brought the two of them so close that the perpetual sense of nausea which she had suffered since leaving home was suddenly heightened and she found herself retching painfully, her hand across her stomach. It reminded her of how she used to feel when she was pregnant, only that this lasted all her waking hours.

At night she dreamt of home and of people there, dead and alive. Last night she had dreamt of Tommy Murtagh, the youth from her mother's village who had caused such a scandal by running away from home to join the International Brigade. He had been killed in Spain before Martina was born but last night he had come to her, his forehead bound by a bloody bandage, and begged her to take him in.

'I can't,' she had replied. 'I can't take you in – you're a communist and Señor Osca supports General Franco.'

Her life was neither satisfactory nor busy. The empty hours stretched out beyond the city skyline to the arid plains of Castile. She wandered the city like a stray dog, searching in the sea of inscrutable olive-skinned faces for a rosy complexion that would denote a childhood spent exposed to Irish winds. She found the Spaniards distressingly uniform – bland brown eyes, strong white teeth, and the skin, where never a hint of blood peeped through. She couldn't see them as individuals; she couldn't read them or make any sense of the expressions on their handsome faces. She would never be anything but a foreigner here. They stared at her too and she thought they must be viewing her as an oddity – like one of the dwarfs in Velasquez' court paintings. '*Qué raro*,' they would say, '*qué tipo más raro*.'

She had exiled herself in this harsh and alien country for she was too old to be assimilated. Like Ruth, she must endure exile for love, although Ruth at least had had her husband by her side.

She watched how they strutted past, these Spanish men, whose ancestors had conquered the world. *Conquistadores*. Their foreignness was implacable, proclaimed in their raised chins, their thrusting chests. Spanish armies had tramped across the world; Spanish sailors had circumnavigated the globe. Isabel the Catholic had given notice that Spain was the hub of the universe, and for these clerks and shop assistants who now walked through the Retiro, this was still true.

In Dublin, Martina recalled, people walked like crabs. They sidled away, heads bent and not only against the wind. No wonder she had difficulty with the light over here – the vanquished could not look at the sun.

Around her, Spanish voices rang out. In the beginning, surrounded by Spanish conversation, she used to feel as if

150

she were in the middle of machine-gun fire; now she could understand them better but she still found herself cringing from such robust affirmation. Irish voices mumbled and muttered and fell away in dying cadences. Unfinished sentences hung in the air which was thick with ambiguities and uncertainty.

How Martina admired the Spanish style, the panache with which they faced the world. And how clearly she could see that it could never be for her. Exile at least was helping her to define herself, offering her answers for her strange and fractured past. She must accept her status – *extranjera*, stranger. She must learn from it and gain wisdom, and with wisdom might come courage. And with courage?

Gently, gently, Martina. Tread carefully across the bloody stones of Madrid.

Martina looked at her watch. She had half an hour to spare yet before setting out for home. This afternoon, she had to shorten a dress for Marisol and take in Ana's jeans. She had promised Julio, too, that she would take him to the cinema to see a new film about the Vietnam war. Martina had seen more war films since coming to Madrid than she had ever seen in Dublin.

She yawned. There were restful aspects to her new life – no decisions to be made, no responsibilities. She did not have to worry if the roof leaked or if the grass in the lawn grew weedy. She did not have to think about what to cook for dinner, or whether it was time to invite guests along.

She slipped the letter into her jacket pocket and opened her grammar at the chapter on radical changing verbs.

'*Duermo*', she read, 'I sleep. *Sueño* . . . I dream'.

16

The meal had been excellent. They had both had the same: pasta followed by veal and a bottle of Terlano. Now they sat sipping coffee, Robert an espresso and Louisa a *cappuccino*. Since coming to London they had discovered a passion for Italian food and, when they dined out, which they did most nights, more often than not they ended up in an Italian restaurant.

Robert asked for the bill.

'Shall we go home?'

'No. Walkies.'

London still intoxicated them: its vastness, the sense it gave them of being invisible as they walked around its streets. After the confines of Dublin, it released them, making them feel irresponsible and unfettered.

At night they walked for miles, arm in arm, more like lovers than father and daughter. They knew no one. A London-based Persse cousin (dug up with efficiency by the girls as soon as Robert told them they were looking for somewhere to live) had disappeared to a dig in North Africa, leaving them his flat on Primrose Hill at a nominal rent for six months. It was a blessing to have them happen along, he had assured them. What with squatters and burglars, property could not be left empty in London any more.

In the tall house on Primrose Hill their neighbours nodded civilly but kept their distance. They didn't have anyone in to help them run the flat and they received no invitations. They were on their own.

It was as they wanted it, a time and place apart. They were

kind and gentle to one another, each knowing how grievously the other had suffered. Lou brought Robert breakfast in bed; Robert did the shopping and cooked. They went to the cinema together, to concerts, to visit the Tate and the Victoria and Albert Museum. They sat in pubs at lunchtime and drank halves of bitter instead of glasses of beer and remembered to bring the glasses back to the bar if they wanted a refill. London was simultaneously foreign and familiar. It seemed safer than Dublin, cleaner, better tempered.

'Of course I'll go back,' Robert would say from time to time. 'I'm just staying here for the six months.'

'You don't have to – we could always get another flat.'

'No, Lou, you're on your own over here. I don't want it said I moved in with my daughter. Besides, I want to go home eventually. I don't know where I'll go – probably stay with the girls at first.'

The house on the square had been sold. It had been bought by a builder, furniture and fittings included, as the auctioneer put it. Two commercial concerns had been interested but the builder had been tenacious, topping all bids with equanimity.

'Are you going to live in it yourself?' Robert had asked him.

'Of course I am,' Mr McCarthy had replied, sounding insulted. 'This part of Dublin is coming up again, you mark my words. People are getting fed up with those suburban boxes; they're going to start moving back. And everything is so perfect here – your wife had excellent taste.'

'I'm glad you like it.'

'Super. We wouldn't change a thing – except that we'll need an extra bathroom or two. Maureen couldn't live without the jacuzzi. I'll tell you something, Robert – they don't build houses like this any more.'

Robert smiled but Mr McCarthy had spoken without irony.

Robert was rich. For the first time in his life he had more money than he could think of ways of squandering it. Meticulously he had made Mr McCarthy give him two cheques, one for the house and a separate one for the contents. This was lodged in a bank in Martina's name.

The row of noughts at the end of his own cheque had made him laugh. 'You'll be a rich woman some day, Lou.'

'No. You must spend it, Dad.'

'How? Can you see me in a blazer and peaked cap on a yacht in Monte Carlo?'

'You could travel.'

'I don't want to, not further than Paris, anyway. I don't think the money is going to make any difference.'

It did, of course; most importantly, it allowed Robert to rid himself of the gallery, surrendering the lease and giving those paintings which he owned away – one to Mr McCarthy, which touched the builder's granite heart. In other respects it conferred on him the freedom of spontaneous indulgence. Now, in restaurants, he opened the wine list at the more expensive end – he and Lou were fast becoming connoisseurs. In the street he could flag down a taxi without thinking about the cost. He bought nothing for himself – his lack of interest in possessions hadn't changed, but he showered gifts on Louisa. He brought home bottles of scent, records, a sophisticated Japanese camera. He searched through junk and antique shops and presented her with an eighteenth-century snuff box and a pretty enamelled egg, which might have come from the Russian Imperial Court, except for the price tag.

'Stop it, Dad. Stop giving me things.'

'But it gives me pleasure.'

Louisa, seeing the pain in his eyes, softened. 'Me too, Dad, but remember, I'll have to cart everything off when I move in a couple of months.'

She worried about him, what he would do, rattling around on his own in Dublin. She thought, but only fleetingly, of giving up college: that would simply add to his worries.

Robert, however, knew himself to be on the mend. He was still fragile but increasingly he felt (and he admitted it to himself now) a sense of relief.

He had begun to admit other things, too – that business about Dr Morgan, for example. He must have known that no amount of family therapy was going to weave them into a family once again. It had begun to break up naturally, in any case; Lou would be spending less and less time at home and when she did return it would be in her new alien status as an adult. As for himself and Martina . . .

The sense of loss was still there, but less acute now. The dull ache of her absence would linger, probably for ever. Since Charlotte's death, however, Robert had begun to realize that life was a series of partings.

He hadn't thought to have been so radically changed by her death. Alive, she had seemed little more than a nuisance most of the time and, although he had tolerated her with ease, for that was his temperament, it had been many years since he had felt any affection for her. He tried to remember how he had felt when his father had died. Relatively unaffected, he imagined. At eighteen, it had seemed the natural order that someone of sixty-two should suddenly snuff it.

Now, he saw his own mortality in Charlotte's. He was aware of the brutal and careless finality of death, its even-handed indifference.

He tried, without success, to summon up some belief in an afterlife. As one who had quite enjoyed church services, finding the sermons soothing and the hymns invigorating, he now realized that he didn't believe in any old man with a white beard, any Father who had a divine plan for him and Charlotte, for Martina and Lou. Dead was dead: Charlotte and the dodo, both of them extinguished for ever.

They were a tough lot, though, the Persses. He was reminded of his grandfather who had survived the Somme and had died literally with his boots on, falling down the stairs at eighty-two, a Romeo and Julietta still clenched between his teeth. A great-aunt, Mary-Jane Robinson, had died with her boots on too, her demise being even more picturesque. One Christmas Eve, furious because the cook and maid had both walked out, and wanting to teach everyone a lesson, she had stuck a broom up the drawing-room chimney and climbed up after it. She had got stuck halfway up, which had brought on a heart attack, an ever-present danger, according to family history, in one of her choleric temperament. When her husband came in some two hours later he had seen her button boots dangling over the fireplace.

'And she had the daintiest feet in the county,' he kept repeating to those who came afterwards to offer their condolences.

And how would Robert remember Charlotte? What would he say of her in years to come? They had lived in the same house for some twenty-five years, in the same city for almost fifty, but all that time had been blotted out for Robert. When he thought of Charlotte now, he recalled no childhood anecdotes, no family outings, no rows nor celebrations, neither her ebullience nor her infuriating mannerisms – all of this had been annihilated, his childhood, his manhood, by Martina's single monstrous deed.

It was not a question of forgiving his wife, that didn't really arise, but he could not make himself forget.

The past was irretrievable and Martina, he now believed, belonged to the past. He had determined to make a new life for himself when he sold the house and, whereas initially the prospect had filled him with dread, tremulously, he had recently begun to feel its appeal. There were books to be read, music to be listened to, pictures to be viewed, fields to be walked, mountains to be climbed. Even women to be admired.

He was glad of the dark, which concealed his features from his daughter. That random thought seemed both illicit and delicious. Last Thursday a young woman had called at the flat, looking for his cousin. She had lingered, even when she learned of Maurice's absence, and afterwards Lou had said, 'You were certainly getting the eye.' Robert had laughed, protesting her youth, but in bed that night he found himself remembering the thrust of her thigh against his as she had turned to face him on the sofa. And scent. And soft eyes that looked at him with hesitancy and expectation.

There was still a sense of disloyalty when he thought of other women but there was also a sense of relief – at least he was still functioning normally.

'I'm not even tired,' Louisa said, running up the steps in front of him. 'These night walks are good for us, Dad; I'm sure we'd both be fat as fools without them. Would you like a cup of something?'

'No, I think I'll go straight to bed.'

He turned the key and stood back to let her in.

'Post!' Louisa bent down. 'For me – no, for both of us. Look, Dad.'

Together they stood and stared at the square blue envelope with the foreign stamp. It had been re-directed from Dublin and was rather dog-eared. Robert let it rest on the palm of his hand. Quite plump and addressed in a familiar hand to Louisa and Robert Persse.

Robert put it in his pocket.

'Go and make that tea, Lou. I'll draw the curtains and turn on the heat. I think it's got a bit nippy.'

When Louisa came back with a tray, he was sitting on the sofa. The lamps were lit and the gas fire was already scattering the evening chill. On a table in front of Robert lay the blue envelope. He patted the sofa and tentatively, even a shade reluctantly, perhaps, took up the letter.

'Sit beside me, darling, and we'll read this together. I knew Mummy would get in touch. Haven't I always told you, Lou, how much she loves you?'

17

When Louisa closed her eyes the noise and movement of the train were transformed and she seemed to find herself skipping along, once again part of the snake formation that writhed its way around the streets of Pamplona. The tinny music of the bands washed into the crevices of her ears and her hips swayed in time to their beat.

But San Fermín was not what it used to be – for the past week everyone she had met kept on telling her so. The solemn young Americans, the middle-aged hippies, all seemed to want to convince herself and Bick – whose first *fiesta* it was – that things had been going downhill for years; in fact, since Hemingway had written about it it had lost its purity and become just another tourist attraction. The bulls were poor specimens, the matadors poorer still. As for the crowds that lined the streets and slept in doorways and on café tabletops, these lacked the stature of the revellers of old who never slept during the entire week and sustained themselves on gallons of red wine and yards of *chorizo* sausage.

'Come to San Fermín,' Bick had said in London. 'A friend wrote me from the States and he says he can't make it this year but we can have his room. He goes every year and he books this room for the next *fiesta* when he's leaving. Do come, Lou. I want you to experience the beauty and the art of the bullfight. When it's well done it's – it's orgasmic.'

In the windless, crimson bullring, Louisa had experienced no sexual or other thrill. She looked coldly at the ancient spectacle unfolding in front of her, at the chanting crowd working itself into a state of near hysteria. The band jangled on, the sun stood still overhead and a small black bull ran into the ring and stared balefully around.

'I think he's a good one,' Bick shouted into her ear. 'Look how he stands, his pride. Yes, he's a *toro bravo*, for sure.'

She thought she hated the picador most for he was not as easily dismissed as the boy matador who stamped his tiny feet at the bull, play-acting in gaudy costume and pigtail. The fact that the picador was on horseback lent him a spurious dignity and authority. After he had withdrawn his lance from the bull's neck and turned an unsmiling face towards the crowd, she could feel his arrogance willing her to be impressed, to take him seriously.

By the time the fifth bull had been killed she had ceased to feel indignant and was merely bored.

'I'm not going to any more fights,' she told Bick.

'Ah, come on, Lou – you've got to. You're just feeling like this because it's your first fight. I bet you felt sorry for the bull.'

'Not particularly.'

'But that's the wrong focus. Look – I've got some books in the *pensión*, we can read them together and it'll help you understand.'

'Bick – *you* understand. I'm not going to any more bull-fights. You go if you want to, I'm not stopping you.'

For the rest of the week they spent their nights on the streets of Pamplona. They moved from bar to bar, eating *tapas*, drinking red wine from goatskins, joining the surging mass of bodies that heaved its way through the streets. They danced and sang and Bick got himself a red beret and neckerchief and pretended that he, too, was Basque.

In the mornings, with the arrival of first light, they squeezed themselves into a doorway or on to a balcony to watch the running of the bulls. The men and boys who had danced and sung and drunk all night now ran in front of the bulls who, corralled by the steers, thundered through the narrow streets. Sometimes someone fell, inches from the curving horns. One morning a young Dutchman was gored and by afternoon rumours were circulating that he had died on the way to the hospital.

When the bulls were safely locked up, Louisa and Bick returned to their *pensión* where they slept until two in the afternoon, lunchtime. Then, when all the world was making its way to the Plaza del Toros, they climbed the stairs, hand in hand, and, in the quiet of their room, in its shuttered green light, they made love.

It had been a good week, a success, but Louisa didn't think, somehow, that she would marry Bick. In a way she loved him, his strong brown body, his gentle, biddable temperament, but she could not see herself married to someone who described things as orgasmic.

Still, she missed him now, sitting alone on this train that was carrying her over the mountains to deposit her in two hours' time in a seaside village at her mother's feet.

Or perhaps she was just feeling nervous. A whim had set her on this journey. When Bick had suggested the Pamplona festival she had thought: Yes, and I could visit Mother just along the coast.

Robert had not been enthusiastic. 'Is there any point, Lou, really?'

'I just thought.'

'We don't even write any more. I don't see the point, but if you feel you must, then go ahead, darling.'

During the four years since Martina's departure, their lives had become separate and adjusted.

Robert had not gone back to Dublin. He had bought a house in Oxfordshire, small and modern. For the last nine months he had been sharing it with an industrial chemist, a forthright Englishwoman who washed her face with soap and water and loved Robert with equilibrium.

When Louisa went to spend weekends with them, she found the atmosphere relaxing. Robert did the cooking and cleaning and Hilary's gaze followed him around, her brown eyes behind her glasses lit with pride and affection. They played tennis together and took Hilary's cocker spaniel for long, ambling walks. Robert had grown plumper and rather untidy. When he boasted that he intended never to wear a collar and tie again, the industrial

160

chemist in her neat blouse and skirt smiled fondly at him while complaining to Louisa that she could do absolutely nothing with him.

As for Louisa, she had quite grown up. The loneliness of her childhood had stood her in good stead so that she didn't tremble among strangers nor cry herself to sleep in her narrow bed at night.

At college she worked hard and was popular. Her fellow students found her a good sort – dependable but fun. Nobody, however, took liberties with Louisa Persse. She was watched with interest by her teachers, for opinion had it that this girl might one day amount to something.

She had been motivated to make this trip by a mixture of curiosity and compassion. Four years ago, when Robert, after the arrival of Martina's first letter, had offered his daughter irrefutable proof of her mother's madness, Louisa had felt a great burden of guilt lift from around her neck. It had hung there, unrecognized, and then, as it lifted, Louisa had focused not on Martina, but on herself. She had straightened and stretched and, sniffing the air, had thought: So it wasn't my fault after all. I didn't fail her, it just couldn't be helped.

She had not been disgusted by Martina's act and, released from her own guilt, she found that her mother had soon begun to fade. She thought of her less often as she settled in at college. It was as if Martina were dead, but happily dead, freed from such great suffering that her daughter could only rejoice.

Now, as the train chortled merrily along, it seemed to Louisa that she herself must have been mad to have embarked on such a journey. Robert had been right – it was pointless. What would they say to one another? Why had she come? When the bus which had taken her the last five miles finally deposited her, she slunk into its hot metal side, hoping vainly that nobody would be there to meet her.

'Louisa! You haven't changed as much as I expected.' The embrace was tentative, apologetic.

161

'Hello, Martina.'

Martina looked as if she had been struck.

'I'm sorry – I didn't mean anything. I call Dad Robert. Somehow it seems – '

'Of course, it's much more sensible – I approve. I mean, you're an adult now.'

'You've changed.'

'Yes, I know I look much older.'

'More beautiful.'

Martina blushed.

She wore a faded cotton dress and shabby brown sandals. The skin on her face and arms was a pale biscuity brown. She was much thinner than Louisa remembered and her hair had turned quite white, silvery now in the afternoon sun. She looked old and worn and very beautiful.

They walked side by side through the sandy streets of the little town. Nobody was about and the houses they passed had their shutters closed against the afternoon heat. Music came from the dark mouth of a bar outside which groupings of metal chairs and tables were all deserted.

'The family is away,' Martina said, pushing in a tall gate. 'Sit here on the verandah and I'll bring you some lemonade. I'll show you to your room later.'

Before supper they went for a walk on the beach. They talked of Louisa's life and of Martina's; of London and Madrid and Dublin. Just as they were walking up the shallow steps of the house, Martina asked, 'And how is Robert?'

'Oh, he's great, fine. He's living in Oxfordshire now – but of course you know that. I'm afraid neither of us is a very good correspondent.'

'No, no. You're both busy. I have lots of free time. It's easier for me.'

Wistful Martina, expecting something from this visit which her daughter had never intended. It was better to be frank now, Martina might as well know straight away. 'I think I should tell you – '

'I hope you like Spanish food,' Martina interrupted her. 'I've grown quite fond of it.'

They ate the meal in the kitchen, served by a maid who refused to sit down with them but who chatted away to Martina in Spanish.

'We'll have coffee in my little *salita*. I've got a bottle of Fundador there. Have you tasted Spanish brandy yet, Lou?'

Her mother appeared to have learned to drink since coming to Spain.

'Louisa, darling.' This time the kiss was one of simple affection. 'Don't look so worried. He's met someone, hasn't he?'

'Yes, I was going to tell you – '

'Never mind. I knew it, somehow. I don't mind, really I don't. He deserves another chance.'

Louisa sipped the fiery brandy.

'And what about you, Lou? Any plans?'

'I hope to go to the States next year.'

'A boy?'

'Well, I've got a boy, yes – '

'I'm glad. Just be careful.'

Louisa didn't explain to her mother that, though she would travel to America with Bick, it was not because of him she was going. She was going because of the real passion in her life, because of Georgia O'Keeffe. That was why she planned to travel to New Mexico, to find herself an *adobe* house and paint in the white, squinting light of the desert.

She said, 'It's nothing serious.'

'Maybe not, but these things have a way of developing. When I met your father at a tennis club hop I never thought I'd end up married to him.'

'Oh, Mother.' Louisa sucked air into her mouth in an effort to disguise a sob. 'That brandy is strong stuff. Listen.' She took the small dry hand between both of hers. 'Let's make this a real holiday. Let's have lots of fun and go out eating and drinking every night. Let's have a swim before breakfast. Let's – just enjoy ourselves.'

'Of course we shall.'

'And I'm going to keep in touch – I promise. I'm even going to write regularly.'

It would be pity more than love that would cause her to pick up a pen. She would try to make time in a busy young life because she was a kind girl. But she had no need of a mother any more. And love and need were flowerheads on a single stem.

Rain fell steadily. A summer in Northern Spain could be as treacherous as in Ireland and this morning's rosy promise had been quenched by the arrival of some high-handed clouds at noon.

In her bedroom Martina sat sewing, looking down on the dripping garden. Yesterday morning Louisa had taken a train for Madrid where she intended to meet Bick and travel down with him to Seville. By the end of the week, the family would be back. Since Louisa's departure Martina had been thinking of her own parents and their short lives. Her father was dead at fifty, her mother at sixty-five. If she were to fulfil the prophecy of her genes, she did not have much time left – fifteen, twenty years?

She looked down at the brass thimble on her middle finger, feeling its looseness. It had been Bridie's, worn by her all her life, and here it was today, continuing on its foolish, useful existence.

She took it off and placed it on the table in front of her to ponder its awful significance. It, a cheap poor thing, produced without thought or care, still existed, while the warm quick flesh which had so often filled it was no longer there; nor probably now the bone that had supported that flesh.

She was shaken by the monstrousness of her realization, more monstrous by far than indifference or ingratitude or love outgrown. Or the desecration of someone's grave.

She rose and stretched and felt a healthy animal response from a body used to walking ten miles at a time. Leisure and isolation threw up unasked-for rewards.

She opened the window and thrust out her head. Turning her

face upwards she felt and tasted the rain, aware with every nerve in her body of the overwhelming and mysterious seductiveness of the material world.

She withdrew her head and shook off the raindrops, laughing.

Nothing made sense but she was suddenly ravenously hungry. She would cook herself some sardines, huge and succulent, caught this morning in the Bay.

And tomorrow?

Tomorrow she would laugh at the gods of creation, inviting them to do their damnedest.